Those eight hours with her

Anjum Awasthi Malik

Invincible Publishers

First Printing: 2019

ISBN: 978-81-942799-0-7

Invincible Publishers

Registered Address: 201A, SAS Tower, Sector 38, Gurgaon - 122003

Printed in India by Excel Printers Pvt. Ltd.

Dedicated to my husband

Present Day

September 2019

Grand Finale, *The Singing Star*

Mumbai

My hand automatically goes over my wife's hand, as the host invites the three finalists of the reality show, *The Singing Star*. My wife entwines her fingers with mine and clenches them to pass her strength to me. Her eyes dart at me instantaneously, sensing the nervousness I am oozing at this moment. My heart beats so erratically and irrationally that I doubt I am having a silent heart attack.

"She is going to win. Stop worrying." She says confidently and smiles at me. I blink my eyes in response, tightening my grip on our joined hands. I look up at the stage as the three finalists enter. My gaze spontaneously trains on my princess, Nitya. Seeing her dolled up in a blue gown with a tiara on her head, my heart somersaults.

She looks so beautiful.

My heart swells with pride as she gracefully stands at the grand stage with her co-contestants. She is a true epitome of beauty with brains. I am not saying this just because she is my daughter; I am saying this because she deserves this title. In a short period, she has gained a considerable fan following. I won't be surprised if soon she has more followers than me.

The host compliments Nitya with the words that mirror my thoughts. She smiles in response and twirls to show her attire. Her long hair that cascade down to her waist in loose curls, fans around as she gyrates. Her eyes are glittery with a tint of blue that makes her look like a mermaid. With the entire make-up and dress-up, she is looking older than her actual age. I join my hands and bring them to my mouth in an attempt to hide my apprehension. I have never felt this anxious in my entire life. Not even when it was my first performance on the stage. Opposite to my state, my princess is standing there all confident and poised.

I love her so much! I throw a silent flying kiss at her. I can move mountains for her, but this delay in announcing the result is sapping all the patience out of me.

Why can't the host just declare the results? Why he has to bring up everything and anything here? I know I am thinking ridiculously, but it's something I really can't help. Anchor announces something that my mind fails to register amidst all the thoughts running in my head. The big screen at the back of the stage starts playing a film showing the journey of three finalists in the last three months.

Now that's something I can watch again and again. It's a treat to witness how my little girl has mellowed in just a few months. She has been so benevolent yet rivalrous towards her companions throughout the journey of *The Singing Star*. She competed with her fellow participants with such determination that left me dumbfounded many times. I guess she has inherited her resoluteness from her mother along with the looks.

The film starts with long queues of kids waiting for their turn during the audition and then various kids showcasing their talents in front of the judges and a swarm of audience. A smile tug on my lips as the screen shows my baby girl's first performance.

Does she have to go through these numerous gruelling auditions to get a chance to sing on a big platform? That, when her father owns one of the biggest music bands in India? The answer is a big *no*, but she wanted to do it without any help from me, and I let her, even though it broke my heart a little. I have promised my daughter and my wife that I would stay out of it. They also went to the extent that nobody here knows that she is my daughter. According to them, it would have influenced the public voting.

I hear the sniffing beside me. One look at my wife and I know she is going to have a meltdown any moment. This event is much more special for her than me. After all, she has worked as hard as Nitya. I wrap my one arm around her shoulder, and she leans into my touch. She is the most selfless and loving woman I have ever seen. We both look back at the stage with ever-rising curiosity.

Once the film was over, the whole venue applauds with loud thunder.

"While we wait for the results, I request to our talented little munchkins to perform the last song of this season," I hear the host saying. I watch it happen in slow motion as my princess, along with two others, takes centre stage and start singing a song that takes me back to the evening that had changed my life entirely. My vision blurs carrying me away from the moment as my mind slowly starts reeling the events that make me stand where I am standing today in my life.

CHAPTER 1

Down The Memory Lane

December 2010.

New Year Eve

Rock Concert, New Delhi.

"Now we are going to invite on stage the star of this evening. Are you ready for him?" I heard the hostess's voice from backstage. The crowd that was already frantic, went even more insane. It was so loud that I fought the urge to stick my fingers in my ears.

"Hang on, guys. I don't think Ady heard you. If you want him on stage right now, then call his name louder," she said. It was not even possible to get louder, but the crowd did as it started chanting my name.

"Ady, Ady, Ady,"

They even stomped their feet, waved their hands, and whistled. They say once you are in the limelight, you get used to it, but nothing would ever get me used to the thousands of people gathered just for a glimpse of mine. It was so overwhelming. I looked at my bandmates, who have already taken their positions after the individual introductions by the host. Who could believe the four roommates that started playing music just for fun, would end up being one of the fastest rising music band that was adored by the youngsters.

Riyaz, that's the name of our band. After the hard work of several years, we burst into the limelight two years ago when one of our songs went viral on YouTube.

Let me introduce my bandmates here. Shaunik, aka Shaun, has a great hand when it comes to drumming. He plays the drum so effortlessly as if the sticks dance on his fingers. Niketan aka Nik is a hell of a bassist I ever came across. He could also write a song like nobody's business. And Manik—he is a past master at playing the guitar and could do rap in a trice to add his touch to the song. Many other members got added to our team, but we four are the soul of *Riyaz*. I may be the lead singer of our band, but I am nothing without my team.

Call it a coincidence that we ended up in the same room in the hostel during our graduation. Initially, we sang just for fun. A stupid Rock band competition at our college was enough to make us realize our passion for the music. We never stopped after that. We took every opportunity that came our way. Be it performing in night clubs and bars or private parties. Initially, we did it for free, but soon it became the source of our income. The journey wasn't that smooth, though, but I believe the real testing happens on the rough road.

The stage lights dimmed, and I knew it was time for my entry. I bowed at the first step as I set my foot on the stage. My bandmates played the intro music as the spotlight aimed at me. I started the show with our most loved song, and the crowd went wild. The flickering lights were so blinding that I couldn't see the audience, just a vague outline of figures swaying, but the enthusiasm of the audience was palpable as they sang along with me. I didn't know how the next one-hour got blurred while singing to the crowd. The whole auditorium roared with the whistles and claps as I sang the last note of the song. I removed the microphone and looked at the audience in front of me. Whoever said dreams are just dreams, they have nothing to do with the reality, should see this moment. I was the living example to prove them wrong. I wouldn't say I have achieved everything I wanted, but looking at the audience waving and screaming my name, seeing me standing in front of them made me gratified. Once the arena lit up with the light, my eyes wavered at the crowd randomly searching for someone. The same pang of disappointment surged my heart when I couldn't find the one I had been searching for the past six years. I smiled and waved at the boisterous crowd as I scampered off the stage, exhausted and dripping in sweat.

"Ady, Ady, Ady, Ady,"

The whole auditorium roared in cadence as I wiped the sweat off my face backstage. I twisted the cap of the water bottle as I headed towards the dressing room. After playing some last beats for the audience, the rest of my team members joined me there after a few minutes. We had two hours break before we would be playing for the audience again for the midnight celebrations. After us, the stage was taken over by some dance troupe.

"Ady, you got any plans?" Shaun asked, watching me taking out my wallet from the locker, while Nik and Mani poured themselves a glass of wine.

"Just need some fresh air. I will be back before our next performance," I said as I put my jacket on.

"Do you want me to come with you?" He asked, knowing well my answer. He knew that I always needed this alone time after the show.

"Nah... I will be fine. You relax here," I said over my shoulder as I took my leave. I walked outside the auditorium and pulled the brim of my ball cap down. It wasn't like people recognized me all the time, but when you are outside the place where you have just performed, chances are quite high. As I exited the venue, the frigid waft of December caressed my face and tried to creep under my clothes. Unwelcoming, I zipped my jacket and tugged my hands in the pockets.

Hoping to find an isolated place, I wandered on the road. I needed a place where I could steal a moment for myself and rest the gushing thoughts cramming my mind, which was unlikely to happen. Delhi is gruelling any day of the week, but it has to be totally brutal when it's New Year eve.

I didn't know why, but after every performance, I had this urge to be alone. I was what I had always yearned to be, yet I felt that something was missing. Something I couldn't put my finger on, but I knew it troubled me incessantly.

A broken promise or more like a forgotten promise.

And there came the thought I wanted to evade. Even after six years, since we parted our ways, she still crammed my mind like no one else. Six years back, she had promised to call me when I would get my first taste of success. Since then, after every performance, I waited for her call; I looked into the crowd hoping to see her amidst the audience. But that day never came. I knew I was expecting too much. You can't expect someone to keep a promise just after spending a few hours with him or her. I would be surprised if she even remembered my name, leave alone, my number. She never gave me her contact number. Wasn't that the first clue that she didn't want me in her life? Or maybe it was her way to push me towards the path that led me to where I was today.

My heart sank, thinking she might have forgotten me when there wasn't a day I hadn't had a wandering thought about her. I shook my head to purge her out of my mind. She was never for me. She was akin to the sun—the only one in the sky... and sadly alone. People either appreciated her warmth or carped about her fieriness. But she kept spreading her light on everyone who came her way. Anyone who got a fragment of that light assumed her to be theirs, but she belonged to no one. She was a free bird, where I was the prisoner of my own desire and dreams. Lost in my thoughts, I walked around half a kilometer ahead on the road.

The constant honking and buzzing of vehicles swarmed my ears, but my mind was too occupied to register any of them. The hustle and bustle of these big cities never failed to amaze me. Not in the right way, though. Being from calm and serene Dehradun, I found it difficult to acclimate in this kind of environment. Though I had an office in New Delhi too and had been spending more time here lately, that didn't make me like the city. I'm not bragging here, but I am not just the lead singer and lyricist of *Riyaz* but also a successful entrepreneur who had raised his father's business ten folds by now. My father owned a toy factory called *TingTong*. After his demise, the legacy was passed on to me. My parents started it when they realized they couldn't have kids. It was their way to bring all the kids of the town to their shop and lessen the pang of incompleteness. But soon it became my father's passion, and he started his own toy factory, *TingTong*—kids called his shop by this name because of the bell that chimed *Ting-Tong* every time someone entered in the shop. In no time it became a household name because of the superior quality, excellent variety and safest designs for the kids. Just not only in Dehradun but also all over the northern region in India. He wanted to expand his business further but was afraid to take the risk. When he came to know that my mother was pregnant with me, he took it as a positive go-ahead sign. Having me was no less than a miracle for them. I smiled, remembering my dad who used to say: '*We made every little heart happy around us, and that's why angels smiled at us and gifted us you.*' As a kid, I actually believed that angels came down to handover me to my parents.

As I took the left turn, I saw a shopping complex packed with various restaurants and clubs. I absent-mindedly padded towards one of the restaurants. It wasn't grand, but what enticed me was the open terrace arrangement with live karaoke. Aiming to get a glass of beer or two, I took the table at the farthest end, finding it unoccupied surprisingly. Even though the place was packed, the crowd seemed decent as the families occupied most of the tables.

I ordered a beer with some light snacks. I heard someone singing an old song on the karaoke. I hummed the song along with the singer as I remembered the lyrics by heart. As he got down the stage after finishing the song, one of the staff members challenged... or say encouraged the occupants to sing more songs. Expecting no one to recognize me, on an impulse I took over the stage. I kept my cap on, just in case, but people were more engrossed in eating than noticing who was singing.

I kept singing the song one after another. None of them was mine. Sometimes it's fun to act like an ordinary guy who loves to hum the classic numbers. At least people don't judge you for the lyrics or music or even your singing. Most of the songs written by me were heartfelt rather than the party numbers, whereas Nik was the one to write fast numbers. And that was the reason people often thought of me as someone with a broken heart. Whereas the reality was, I had never been in love. Thinking about this, her name again rang in my mind. I didn't know what kind of relationship I shared with her. I couldn't give any name to it. Some relationships are not defined by a name but by the way they alter your life. I had spent just a few hours with her, and I was never the same again. She made me see the world in a whole different light.

Bringing myself back, I picked the lyrics of the song again. I went on and on. I noticed people who had slowly started paying attention to me, which said to me that I was doing well. I looked up at the sky as I crooned the higher notes and then lowered my gaze slowly. And that was when it happened.

Time stopped as my eyes met with *hers*. Everything around me started disappearing as if I was all alone standing there with my gaze fastened with hers—the one who had always been in my thoughts but was never present physically. After the lapse of six years, she was finally standing in front of me. A slow smile crept on my face. She, too, had recognized me. Her face said it all. She had always been easy to read. Her eyes couldn't hide the surprise… or shock as if she couldn't believe it was actually I. Her lips parted just slightly. The brows furrowed and eyes glassy. She stood there motionless same as me. The world around us suddenly became nonexistent. She was in black trousers and a black shirt. Her hair tied neatly in a bun but covered by a cap same as mine. The drinks she was holding in a tray wavered as her hands shook slightly. Once the initial stigma was gone, I was again aware of my surroundings. And then it dawned on me that she worked in this restaurant. Seeing her working as a waitress induced uncountable questions in my head.

"Riya."

Before I could stop myself, her name slipped out of my lips and ricocheted in the air. She straightened her back as if she just came out of the daze and pivoted, clearly avoiding me. Without caring about the people around us, I scurried off the stage to follow her.

"Riya," I called out again. She stopped but didn't turn.

"I am sorry, sir. But I think you are mistaken. I am not Riya," she said once I came face to face with her. Dodging me, she headed towards the table where she was supposed to serve the drinks. My phone started vibrating in my pocket. I took it out to find Shaunik's call. I looked at the time and realized that time had ticked away really fast.

"Hey," I responded.

"Hey, we have an appearance in twenty minutes. You better be here soon."

"Yeah, I am on the way," I lied and clicked the call to end. There was no way I was heading back without talking to her. Pocketing my phone, I followed her once again. I had already wasted six years, I couldn't waste any more time.

"It's you, Riya. I could have recognized you with all my senses gone." I said as I jogged to be on her heel.

"I repeat, you are mistaken, sir," she said without throwing a second glance at me.

"Why are you working here? Is your so-called dad creating some problem again?" I asked as I walked beside her, watching her warily for some emotion on her face that could tell me I wasn't wrong. She laughed humorlessly and then replied, "Sir, you are just wasting your time and mine too. I am not the one you are looking for." I was about to ask her another question when my phone started ringing again. Groaning, I decided to ignore it. Before I could turn the call down, she loped inside a room where the only staff was allowed. I looked down at the screen that flashed Nik's name, and I instantly knew I was in trouble.

"Hey, you better be here in five minutes. We are heading to the stage, and Shaunik is getting the anxiety attacks. He is super angry,"

"I am coming, Nik. Just handle him for some time anyhow," I said. I left the restaurant, promising myself to come back once the show was over. I had already lost her once; I was determined not to repeat history.

When I came back to the auditorium, my team was already on stage playing the music of one of our super-hit song, while Shweta, our offset backstage singer had taken over the stage. She had always been a good entertainer and a good friend too. As soon as they came to know about my arrival, Shweta wrapped up the song fast and announced that I would be taking up the stage. The crowd roared in ecstasy, and my hand instinctively went to my heart. In moments like this, I felt like I had gotten from life more than what I deserved. But then I reminded myself, I had worked my ass off to reach the place where I was today, and I deserved every bit of it. I bowed before stepping up the stage again. It was my usual stance—my way to thank god for acknowledging my hard work. Wasn't I lucky? Some people never get to see what they have dreamt of, even after putting all their efforts. God blessed me with this day, and I was never going to take it for granted. As I entered the stage, the spotlight followed my path and fans went wild once again.

"Having fun Delhi?" I asked the crowd, and everyone roared and flapped their hands up.

"My apologies for being late here, I know my team covered it well, but I have learnt to take the responsibilities of my deeds," my voice echoed in the auditorium and audience went silent except hushed murmurs here and there curious to know what I was about to talk. "Today, I want to share something with you all. You have always been keen to know about the girl in my life. You often associate my songs to that imaginary girl in your head. Today, I am going to talk about her," I added and again heard the crowd whooping in excitement.

"There was a girl, long ago, who was too special to me, but before I could fathom what it was between us, she left me with a promise to call me once I would achieve a name in the singing. She never did, and I still wait for her call,"

"Awww..." the audience responded in cadence.

"Today, I saw her again. But the timings were too bad that I had to let her go because I didn't want to disappoint you all. The song that I am going to sing next is the one I had written for her long ago, and she knows that this song is for her. Will you all help me to reach it to her? So that it could remind her that she hadn't kept her promise?" the entire auditorium erupted into a synchronized affirmation. I didn't know why I did that. I had never engaged myself in any kind of personal conversation with the audience before. But that moment, everything came naturally, and perhaps it was necessary for me to hurl the bulging emotions out of me.

I started singing the only song I had written after spending those few hours with her. I never made this song a part of my album or concert. It was a part of me that I wasn't ready to share with anyone, but that day, it seemed appropriate. I warbled the full song with my eyes closed. I didn't even realize how quiet was the auditorium while I was humming the lyrics I remembered by heart. Once the song was over, I opened my eyes and looked at the audience. It seemed like they had experienced the lyrics. As if they could feel how I felt for her. Did she feel the same way when I had sung this song for her six years ago? She hadn't talked about it then, but somewhere I was curious to know her opinion. I sang some other songs for another twenty minutes. As the midnight approached, all the people from my team and other artists joined the stage. It was my chance to slip away without getting noticed. Shaunik was the only one I informed before leaving, he understood but had several questions in his eyes that I was in no mood to answer. Half an hour later, I reached the same restaurant where I had seen Riya, but I couldn't spot her anywhere.

"Excuse me," I stopped another waitress in an attempt to get to Riya.

"Yes, how may I help you, sir?" she asked.

"Umm… I was looking for another waitress. She was working here around two hours back," I rambled.

"Sir, do you remember her name?" she looked at me.

"Umm… Yes, Riya?" I answered. She looked up for a moment as if to recall if she knew anyone by that name.

"Sir, I don't remember anyone working here by that name. Maybe she is from another shift. But still, if you want, you may ask the manager," she said, pointing towards an office door.

"Sure. Thanks," I said and rushed towards the manager's office. I knocked at the door before opening it. The manager who was busy on a call, lifted a finger at me gesturing he needed a minute. I waited, but my patience was wearing thin with every passing second. I can't lose her this time, I reiterated in my mind. As the manager gestured me to enter the room, I asked without caring about the pleasantries, "Is a girl named Riya working here?"

"May I know what's the matter?" he asked. I knew that if I wanted to drag any information out of him, I needed a strong reason.

"I was here for an hour or so ago. She was serving at my table. By mistake, along with the tip, I left my credit card too in the bill holder," I concocted an instant excuse that didn't sound like a lie.

"Oh! Sure. Let me check once," he worked on the keyboard of his laptop and then after a moment he looked at me. "Are you sure the name was Riya? Because we don't have anyone working here with this name," he asked, raising his eyes from his computer screen.

"I guess it was Riya. Though, I am not sure," I said dejectedly. Was she really her? Or I mistook someone else as Riya?

"Let me check with my staff once," he said and picked up his phone to call someone from his staff. I held my hand up to stop him, "It's ok. I am in a hurry. I will get my card disabled," I said and turned to leave. The crowd outside had already started getting thin. I left the place with a heavy heart. I didn't know if the girl I saw in the restaurant was indeed Riya or not. But if she was Riya, it was clear from her gesture that she still didn't want me. I wasn't going to pester her. If she wanted me, she would have to contact me. Otherwise, just like before I would let her go.

CHAPTER 2

Down The Memory Lane

I was in my apartment in Delhi. It wasn't big, as my mother had made it clear that she wasn't going to leave Dehradun ever, and even I had no plans to get settled in this city, yet it was lavishly styled and had much more amenities a single person would require. I switched on television as I entered my bedroom. The hour hand had just stroked two in the morning. After returning from the restaurant, I came straightway to my apartment. I poured myself another glass of wine before slipping inside the comforter. After my encounter with Riya—or a girl who looked like Riya—it was much needed. Flipping through the channels mindlessly, I switched off the television when no program could take my mind off of that girl. I tried to sleep, but all I could do was toss and turn. It was five in the morning when I finally gave up on sleeping and headed towards the clubhouse to hit the gym.

I pushed my body to its limit on the treadmill to get her out from my mind. Wasn't I doing it from the last several years? But this time it was different. My encounter with her had reopened all those windows that I had worked hard to shut. Pounding my feet along with the blaring music hammered in my ears as I increased the speed and ran through the final stretch. I was huffing when I turned the treadmill off. Sweat began rolling off my back as I started working out on the bench press. Even after spending an hour there, it still couldn't bait my mind. I had to know what had happened. She had told me once that destiny had brought us together to play a role in each other's life. She had already played hers in mine, and perhaps this was my chance to do something for her. But how could I help her? When she wasn't even ready to recognize me!

I felt frustrated, having no way to reach her. Esha! Maybe Esha could tell me something about her. I pulled out my phone and called Ekta instead, Esha's elder sister. I was more close to her than Esha.

"Hey, Ady. It's such a lovely surprise," she said in her morning voice, and I cringed. It was too early to call someone.

"I am sorry, Ekta. I hope I am not disturbing,"

"Not at all, what is it?" she asked.

"Remember that girl Riya? We met at your wedding?" I asked as if I was asking about her for the first time.

"That hippie girl? Oh Ady, are you still not over her? You have asked me about her numerous times in the last six years. I thought you called me to wish New Year," she carped.

"She wasn't a hippie girl," It still stung when someone tried to demean her.

"Okay, what about her now?" she said as if her patience was wearing thin.

"Do you know anything about her? Like where she went after that and what happened to her, anything? Did Esha ever tell you something about her?" I asked, ignoring her yawn.

"No. You know that Esha wasn't her friend. She just clung uninvited to Esha and ruined my wedding." I winced at her views about her. Ekta never liked her, right from day one. "Now tell me why you are asking about her today?" she added.

"Umm… I saw her yesterday," I replied.

"And…?" she asked and exhaled loudly.

"She didn't recognize me," I answered and heard her chuckle in response.

"Wasn't that her typical behaviour? She used people for her benefit and chucked them when she no longer needed them," she said, and I scowled at her words. She might have guessed my annoyance because she sighed and added, "Trust me, Ady. I am saying this because you weren't the only one to ask about her after the wedding. There is a list," she said, and I closed my eyes in exasperation. Calling her was a mistake.

"Ok, then. Take care. Bye," I was about to end the call when I heard her yelling.

"Now you are going to hang up on me just like that? You are still so selfish, Ady. It's my bad. I still expect from you. Anyway, wish you a very happy new year," she said sarcastically.

"I am sorry, Ekta. I had a gig yesterday night. I am just too tired,"

"You still haven't wished me back,"

"Happy new year,"

"Take care, Ady. And don't be a stranger," she said before clicking the call end.

I took the stairs to reach my apartment instead of the elevator. I shoved the key in the keyhole and opened the door. Deciding not to think about her anymore, I started brewing the coffee. I stripped my drenched t-shirt and tossed it in the laundry bag. Turning on the television, I engaged myself in the news headlines. Every news channel flashed the same news regarding the son of a former minister getting married for political alliance. Having no interest in politics, I switched the channel to CNBC. This habit of watching the news with the coffee, I had inherited from my father. He used to do this as a first thing in the morning. News keep you informed and updated—was his dialogue. My phone started ringing somewhere in the house, and I started looking for it with my eyes still on the television screen. I glanced at the mobile screen and found an unknown number.

"Hello," I responded the call. I was greeted with the silence from the other side and then a sigh. My heart skipped a beat. I didn't know how, but I knew it was her.

It's she. My inside warbled with the excitement.

"Hello?" I said once again.

"Is it Adyant Lohani?" A hesitant voice asked from the other side. It was her. There were very few people who called me by my full name, and she was one of them.

"Yeah," I responded carefully, dreading that any more words would make her recoil.

"Hi, it's Riya this side. Hope you remember," she said, and I pictured her crunching her nose as she said that. I released a breath I didn't even know I was holding.

"Of course, we met yesterday too. Hope you remember as well," now as she had admitted, I felt a little confident to throw her line on her.

"Yes, we did. I am sorry I… I was just… umm…" she trailed off and then added, "Confused" .

"It's ok. I understand, it was your workplace," I tried to make her comfortable. I had expected a sarcastic remark from her, but her apologies took me off guard. Riya that I remembered was too reckless, and talking to her now I realized that perhaps I didn't know her anymore.

"I need your help," she said. I knew something was wrong.

"Anytime, Riya. You know I will do anything for you. I owe you this,"

"You owe me nothing, Adyant. But I appreciate your gesture. It's just… I have no one I could seek help from. It's not like I didn't think about… you, when I came here, but I thought you would have forgotten me by now. Meeting you yesterday gave me the confidence to call you today,"

"Oh! There isn't a single day, Riya, when I don't think about you," I said and instantly bit my tongue cursing myself for stepping the line. We didn't share that kind of relationship.

"What's wrong?" I asked immediately to dodge my previous words.

"Can we meet? It's not something I can explain over the call. I need to tell you everything in person," she said.

"Of course! Where do you want to meet?"

"Umm...Outside the same complex, we met yesterday? Is that ok with you? Can you come there before my shift? I work there from five to eleven,"

"Okay. Is four in the evening fine?"

"Umm... four-thirty?"

"Done, anything else?"

"No. Thank you so much. I know I am bothering you, but trust me I wouldn't have called you if it wasn't urgent,"

"I understand, Riya. You don't need to feel guilty about it," I said with a twinge of pain in my heart. I couldn't imagine her sounding so helpless. She was the kind of girl who didn't look up at others for help. Instead, she would carve her own way without thinking about right and wrong. There was something terribly wrong in her life, and I couldn't wait for another few hours to know about it.

"If you want, I can come right now too," I sounded eager, but I didn't care.

"No. The evening is fine. I will be waiting for you there. Bye for now. Take care," she was about to disconnect when I asked, "Is it your number?"

"No, no. It's not mine. I borrowed it from someone else. I don't have any mobile phone with me,"

"And you remembered my number?" I asked, surprised. I didn't know why, but I needed to hear it from her.

"The only thing I remember by heart. Take care, Adyant," she disconnected the phone immediately, leaving me strangled between the bulging emotions. Did she think about me all this time when I assumed she had forgotten me? Keeping my phone back on the table, I rubbed both my hands on my face and turned off the television. My phone buzzed again, but this time it was from my mother. A smile spread over my face as I saw her name flashing on the screen.

"Hey, Maa, Happy New Year,"

"Wish you the same. Too busy these days, Haan? No time even to talk to your old mother," she carped in her soothing voice.

"It's not like that, Maa. You know I had gigs back to back. But leave that. I have something interesting to tell you. Riya called today," I said smiling, not able to hold it.

"Riya? Is it the same girl you met at Ekta's wedding in Manesar? The one you hadn't stopped talking about since that day?" she teased.

"Maa, now you are exaggerating. I just told you once about her,"

"Yes. But your actions talk about her all the time. You think I don't know from where the name *Riyaz* has gotten its origin?"

"Maa!"

"Tell me. What did she say?"

"She wants to meet me. She is in trouble and needs my help,"

"Oh! I hope it's not anything serious. And do help the girl," she said.

"I will, Maa. I am going to take a shower now. Talk to you

later. Bye, love you." I said and disconnected the call. Before I could put my phone down, it buzzed again, but this time it was from our manager, Yash. I had asked him to inform me about the next planned concerts in advance.

"Hey," I answered the call.

"Ady, it's just to inform you that we don't have any gig planned for the next two months. So you are free to concentrate on your *TingTong*. And also we are scheduled to release our next album this year. I hope you will start working on lyrics soon,"

"Yes, I will. Thanks, Yash."

"Last few months had really been gruelling for all of us. This break was much needed," he said, and I couldn't agree more. Back to back concerts in the last three months had sapped the vigour out of us.

"I agree. Anything else?"

"Nothing for now. I won't call you for the next few weeks until it's something related to interviews or something I can't handle. Anyway, are you joining Shaunik, Niketan and Manik for their trip to the Maldives?" He asked, and I cringed remembering I had forgotten entirely about that trip. Though I hadn't confirmed them as I had a business to look after too, still I had considered the option. But now with Riya in the picture, I was going to disavow. After talking to Yash, next, I called Shaunik to inform him that I had cancelled and they could go ahead with their plans. I headed to the washroom for the shower, suddenly feeling calm and relaxed as for two months I just had to look after my business. Keeping my legs in two boats hadn't been easy at all, but it all seemed worth when I was on the stage living my dream. It hadn't been possible if I hadn't met Riya. She might be an ordinary girl for anyone else, but for me, she had been the light when I was going through the darkest path of my life. And she was so effervescent that she didn't even realize she was saving a life.

Present Day

Grand Finale, *The Singing Star*

Mumbai

"Nitya, Nitya, Nitya..."

"Samarth, Samarth, Samarth..."

"Parth, Parth, Parth..."

I am pulled out of my reverie when I hear the audience cheering for their favorite contestants after they all sang the title song of *The Singing Star*. All the three contestants are one ahead of another. Though I haven't observed their performance meticulously, the way audience is cheering, I know they have done well. The events of the past have occupied my mind so much that I forget to cheer for my baby girl. It's the day that will change her life entirely. The same way her mother had altered mine fifteen years ago when I had met her for the first time. Until then, to concede defeat was my only option.

There always comes a time when you hit rock bottom and are left with just two options: either you rise because you have nothing to lose, or you end everything, again because you have nothing to lose. I was in the same predicament fifteen years back, and even though I was determined to end everything, I rose, and it happened because of those eight hours with her. She was no one. I didn't even know her name then. The only thing I knew was—she was trouble, and I had to stay away from her. The day I saw her for the first time was still vivid and clear in my mind as if it all happened yesterday.

CHAPTER 3

Down The Memory Lane

April 2004

Manesar

The fluttering sound of the wind wafted through my window as I revved my car on the road that led to the farmhouse in Manesar. I was there to attend the wedding of my childhood friend Ekta. Our families had been friends for ages. Ekta and I grew up together, and there was a point when our parents wanted us to settle down with each other. But she was more like a sibling to me. My mom and dad would never have missed this wedding had my dad not encountered with an untimely demise. After going through so much upheaval in the past one-month, even I wanted to dodge this wedding, but when I came to know that all of my college friends were coming to this event, I couldn't let this last opportunity slip out of my hand. Maybe I would never see them in the future. Even though they were close to my heart, but letting them go was the best for everyone. I wasn't going there just to meet them, but also to convince them not to let our dream die. Even if I wouldn't be a part of it. Considering the predicament I was in, it was impossible for me to keep continuing as a lead singer of our band.

Our unnamed band then, or say a band that kept changing its name according to the forthcoming events, wasn't that big, yet it had earned a reputation for itself in the city. We had started getting the invitation and offers from the bars, clubs and private parties. We were determined to make it big, but then the crisis happened. My father suffered a stroke that led to his body partially paralyzed and then the demise. He was never the one to stop me from following my dreams; instead, he was the one to bolster me. Because he knew how hard he had to work to live his passion when no one supported him. When I laid my dream in front of him, already expecting him to burst with fury and determined to counter him, he said something that took me entirely off guard. I still remember his exact words: *No one supported me when I wanted to run my own business. Earning money more than our requirement was never in my books, but I earned it for you so that my son doesn't have to face the obstacles in his path that I had encountered. I am with you, and you will always find me in the front seat of your every concert.* His words still reverberated in my head, but, alas! That day never came. He left the world before our band could even launch its first song.

I took the turn, and the greenery all around welcomed me to the farmhouse. The view outside boasted crop fields spanning as long and far as I could see. Away from the tumult of the city, the farmhouse was serene and picturesque. Spread over several acres, it was more like a palace. Our families used to come here for the vacations. Otherwise settled in Dehradun, Ekta's ancestors used to live in this property long back. I parked my car outside the farmhouse along with the other parked vehicles in the line. My heart thumped in my chest as I took out my bag and headed towards the entrance. I didn't know how I was going to face my friends... or say bandmates after disavowing to be a part of the band. My only real interest in being at the wedding was to meet them and convince them not to give up.

Shaunik had already made it very clear that it would either be all of us or just none. Since the day I had announced that I would no longer be the part of the band, they had completely stopped talking to me, as if I was the reason behind this fallout. Well! Whom was I kidding? I was undoubtedly the reason. But what are you supposed to do when you have social obligations. Giving up on the industry my father had started would mean crushing not only his dream but also destroying many families' livelihood. I had to keep up with the industry's commitment. There had been many people depending on this industry, and I couldn't just let them drown because of my personal reasons. I was not angry with my friends' either. Their reactions to my declaration were entirely justified. After all, in pursuit of saving those several homes, I had crushed my friend's dream. It was my chance to meet them and explain to them why I had to choose my father's business over them. I wished I could make them see that I had reached an impasse.

I was sweating profusely. I didn't know if it was because of April heat or just the anxiety. I crossed the main gate and headed to the main hall. As I passed, I heard the rustling of guests, but I didn't know them enough to meet or greet them. Some of them were the recruits to make the arrangements for the event. The sound of laughter and the music that wafted from the room at the far end of the hall told me where I would find the people I was here to meet. I dreaded the impending conversation. I dreaded the outcome of this conversation, but I had to do it.

I wasn't the one to keep things hanging. If I was going for a new start, I had to end the one I had taken previously in my hand. Though ending it was akin to end my own life. I had always thought I was born to sing. The things people called noise; I could hear the music and lyrics in that too. The flutter of wings wasn't just a sound for me; it was a song that embodied freedom. The thundering of clouds never scared me, because all I could hear was music that bestowed courage. I could read the lyrics in people's silence too. It wasn't the blood that was running in my veins but the music. And when I realized that I could no longer pursue something I was born to do, it broke me to pieces. It frustrated me to death because it wasn't how I had envisaged my future. The worst thing was I couldn't even make someone understand my pain. For them, I had no reason to be disheartened. I was born with a silver spoon in my mouth. I hadn't had to do anything other than just to take over my father's business.

And moreover, singing was considered something people did for hobby and not for the living. And what could have been worse? That instead of fighting, I accepted my fate. I gave up on my singing career and took over my father's business to keep him alive.

With my mind crammed with all these thoughts, I walked towards the room. Before I could enter, a loud and husky laugh made me turn my head to look for the source. There was a strange buzz in that laugh that enticed me first, but when I looked in that direction, it kind of surprised me. I saw a girl sitting on the stairs, surrounded by four to five boys. One was smearing mehndi on her hand, and others were making fun of it, which made her laugh again. She folded her stretched long legs, and the little dress she was wearing rode further up her thighs. It wasn't the scene I could expect in the gatherings of our fraternity. Her attire seemed indecent suggestive considering the occasion. Since childhood, we were raised to behave decently, dress up conservatively and be cautious of our surroundings. I didn't intend to eavesdrop; yet fragments of their conversation teased my ears as I walked, occasionally glancing in their direction.

"Hey, You aren't supposed to write your name on my hand," the girl said facetiously, feigning the anger.

"My name belongs to your hand, sweetheart. Haven't you heard, artists are supposed to write their names under their masterwork?" He said flippantly winking at her. "Is that so?" she gibed leaning to him. It was clear from the panorama that those boys were just fooling around her, and she was enjoying the attention. My trance was broken as Ekta, the would-be-bride, along with her sister Esha rushed to me. Both of them hugged me carefully so that their mehndi didn't spoil my shirt or vice versa.

"I am so glad you came here. I thought you wouldn't come," Ekta said, holding my gaze with hers. Even though she tried to hide, but I could still witness the sheen of tears that she veiled tactfully behind her vibrant smile. As it looked from outside, our relationship wasn't that simple. I had broken her heart. Though unintentionally, but just like my other friends, she was my victim too. Though the reason was entirely different.

'*It's hard to forget your first love, Ady. And I have loved you since I didn't even know what love was. You chose not to love me in return, but that won't make me fall out of love. I will always cherish you as my first love. And you have no right to stop me. I can't wait for you any longer as you have put me in this hopeless situation, but I do hope one day you realize what you have lost.*' Her wistful words reverberated in my head that she had said a day before her engagement. It wasn't that I didn't like her, but I just didn't feel the same way for her. I knew it in my gut that she wasn't the one for me.

"How could I not? I am really happy for you," I said genuinely feeling happy for her.

"So am I. Nikhil is the guy for me. It took me some time to realize, but now I know," she said scathingly. I didn't know if it was sarcasm, or she actually felt that way, but I was truly happy for her.

"I am sure he is. Where do I need to put my luggage?" I asked, dragging my luggage to my side. She was about to reply when our conversation was interrupted as the loud laugh again ricocheted in the room. This time all of us stared at the source.

"This girl!" Ekta said, gritting her teeth in angst. Then she looked at Esha who looked down embarrassed.

"Who is she?" I asked, gesturing the girl with my eyes.

"Ask her," Ekta said, narrowing her eyes at Esha. "It's her friend," she added.

"Not a friend exactly. I was at a friend's party the day before I was supposed to come to Ekta di's wedding. I met her there. When she heard me talking about the wedding, she insisted on joining saying that she had never been to a wedding before."

"So our munificent Esha brought her here to ruin my wedding," Ekta said derisively interrupting Esha.

"Ady Bhaiya, What was I supposed to do? I couldn't refuse her. I didn't know then she had such a wild attitude. Now everyone here is reprimanding me. They want me to send her back. How am I suppose to do that?" she said as her eyes glossed with the tears.

"It's ok. She is the girl of loose morals, and you better stay away from that kind of company. That's all we are worried about for now. Forget her. At least she is entertaining the boys in the wedding," Ekta rambled, her voice a bit soft yet sardonic.

"Ady, come I will show you your room. You may freshen up there and then come down to meet everyone." Ekta said.

"It's ok, Ekta. You don't have to. It's your wedding. Go back to whatever you were doing and enjoy your day. Esha will show me my room," I said, darting my gaze from Ekta to Esha, who shrugged in response.

"It's ok, Ady. I want to do it," she responded with a look, I had known better not to argue with. Ekta led the way towards the room upstairs, and I followed her. The girl sitting on the stairs smiled at Ekta as we passed, but Ekta didn't return her smile and kept climbing up. Once out of their earshot, I asked Ekta, "Where are Shaun, Nik and Mani?"

"Haven't seen them since afternoon, must be somewhere outside," Ekta replied, walking ahead of me and glancing back at me occasionally.

"Is the situation worse?" I asked, knowing well she would understand what situation I was referring about.

"It has to be, Ady. You were the one to blaze the trail, and now you are the one to back off," she said, glancing my way intermittently as she entered the hallway.

"I know. I wish my friends could understand me," I said, following her.

"Remember? What did you guys use to say before every performance? '*We want it bad, and we will make it happen.*' It was you to instil this passion in them. How can you expect them not to resent," she said, opening the door of the room. The room was simple yet elegant with white walls and antique wooden furniture. I instantly loved the cozy interior of the room.

"What am I suppose to do now? They are not even picking up my calls," I said, pinching the bridge of my nose to get respite from growing tension.

"Your decision is right, Ady. This industry means a lot to your family, and without your father in the picture, it needs your undivided attention. You can't sail in the two boats simultaneously. You need to make them understand this. It's going to take time, but they will understand one day," she said. She had always been a most understanding and logical person. Her rationality and the way of thinking had always drawn me. This was the reason I usually turned up to her for any suggestions.

"Now you get ready and come down in ten minutes. I will call them downstairs and will make sure they listen to your side considerately," she said, clenching my shoulder to comfort me. And I relaxed a bit to her reassurance. She left the room, closing the door behind. I took my time to shower, and then changed my clothes to a white silk Kurta with blue denim. Combing my hair, I adjusted my spectacles. When I called myself lead singer, one might assume me to look like a rock star—Tall, sturdy with all the muscles at right places and a style to die for, but I was quite the opposite. I had an average height of five-ten with moderate body, fair complexion, my hair typical black cut in short, and spectacles that I wore gave me more of a nerdy look rather than someone cool. My phone buzzed with a text from Ekta. All my friends were there in the hall, and she was asking me to come down. I rolled my sleeves up as I came out of my room. I walked towards the stairs with thousands of thoughts running in my mind. I felt my pulse thunder through my veins as I took the stairs down to the main hall. My phone buzzed again in my pocket, and I looked down to take it out as I turned to the right. That was when I bumped into someone and heard her muttering a curse as she stumbled a few steps back. I didn't see her face, but I did notice the big mehndi stain on the chest of my Kurta. Before I could say anything, I heard her shouting, "Are you insane? Can't you watch your steps? You spoiled my whole design."

Generally, my immediate response in this kind of situation would be the apologies, but the way she swore the curses, I decided against it. Moreover, it wasn't my fault entirely. When I looked at her face, my response came altogether unexpected.

"I am sure there are plenty of people here ready to redo it for you. So you got nothing to worry," my voice sounded rude even to my ears. Why? I couldn't decipher. Maybe I was seeing her from Ekta and Esha's perspective. She kept looking at me with her mouth slightly ajar, but nothing came out of it, and then she looked down. I instantly felt bad when she just murmured an apology without looking at me. I strained my neck as I watched her back walking away from me but didn't say anything. I looked at the big green spot on my Kurta. Shaking my head, I strode back to my room to change my clothes, silently promising myself to apologize to her for my rude remark later.

Soon after, I was in the hall amidst the people who were everything to me. It stung deep in my gut when I found them snubbing me. They didn't even care for the pleasantries, as if I was an unknown. Overlooking their coldness, I still tried to participate in the ongoing conversation. The environment suddenly got thick with my involvement, and they started to disperse.

"Are you guys going to ignore me for the rest of your lives? As if I am no more alive," I asked, raising my voice and making them snap their gazes at me. "Can we at least talk like mature people for some time here? Rather behaving like petulant kids?" I asked again as I had their attention now.

"Do you have something to say that you haven't said already?" It was from Shaunik as he walked aggressively towards me. The annoyance in his voice startled me. I still wasn't used to his impertinence.

"No," my answer was honest. There was nothing new I was going to tell my bandmates.

"Then, there is no need to repeat the same things again and again. You wanted to walk out, we are letting you. End of the story," he grated the words out, standing a foot away from me.

"I want to tell you that you can still pursue the plan. Even without me. You guys don't have to give up,"

"Are you done? We do not doubt your sanity, so keep your lectures to yourself," It was from Manik.

"Look, Ady, we started it together. And you know well that we are nothing without each other. So it's happening only if we all are into it together. No more discussions," Shaunik passed the final verdict with authority in his voice. His hand clenched at his sides and eyes red in rage... or maybe a disappointment.

"Hey guys, cool down! Just try to think once from Ady's perspective. He has just lost his dad. You think it's easy for him to let you guys down," Ekta piped in. She turned to look at Shaun. "I have seen him singing with guitar in his hand since he was just five. I have seen him breathing music. Do you have any idea how hard it is for him to take this decision? All he needs at this moment is support from his friends. Can we stand with him in his tough time?" Ekta reasoned, and I could sense the tension oozing out of their bodies momentarily, but soon they turned and walked away from me.

"Give them some time, Ady. It's tough for them too," Ekta said, and I responded with a slight bob of my head. "Have you met my parents?" she asked.

"Not yet. I was going to meet them next," I replied.

"Come with me. Nikhil's parents are here too. I will introduce you to them too," she said and took me to them. After meeting everyone, I spent some time there, but the awkward glances that I shared with my friends made me uncomfortable. Seeking some respite from the rising tension, I came out in the lawn outside. The sun was ready to set that made the sky appear orange. I walked to the backside of the house where I knew I could find a lonely and peaceful place. The lights flicked before they came to life to make it luminous as it was twilight. I took in the adorned house that held my beautiful childhood memories. Amidst the green paddy fields, the white farmhouse building studded with lights looked like a royal palace. I sat on the wooden bench as I reached my secret place, which was quiet as compared to the clamour on the other side of the building. I sighed into the welcoming silence, was grateful that I could escape for some time from the conversation that would result in nothing but exasperation. The sound of the fresh and crispy summer wind made the trees sway and rustle. Time blurred at a faster pace as I sat there and stared at the long and endless green fields waning in the darkness. I had always found this place so tranquil that I could easily get lost here. The faded sound of music played by the DJ wafted outdoor, but it couldn't distract me from the serenity of the panorama outside.

It was stupid, but sometimes I felt like if I could get few buttons from the keyboard, like delete, undo, backspace or escape in life too, it would have been so easy. But life doesn't go that way. No matter how difficult the path is, you have to cover each inch on your feet. You keep on walking because somewhere you know that a beautiful destination is waiting, that will make this arduous journey worthwhile. But this hope can be a delusion if you are on the wrong path. I didn't know if the way I had chosen for myself was right or wrong. I just went with the flow, and it felt right. I was just walking on the path other people had laid for me. I had no idea where I was heading, and that despondent thought was killing me. A text on my phone hauled me out of the reverie, It was from Ekta again asking me to join them for dinner. Reluctantly, I stood up to accompany them. I took the long way to reach there to stall my encounter with my friends again. As I took the first turn, I heard her voice again. I didn't need to turn to look at whose voice it was. Her voice embodied the sound of a subdued storm that was hard to ignore.

I was stunned to find her in that discrete place, but one look and I knew she wasn't alone there. It was difficult for them to spot me where I was standing. They kept on talking unaware of my presence.

"Now that was a complete turn off for me," she said, scrunching her nose as she took the cigarette from the boy standing next to her. She puffed on it without flinching and blew the smoke out through her mouth and nose. The boy stepped a little closer to her as they shared a cigarette together.

"Why? People often consider it a good deed," the boy replied.

"Good deed my foot! Like seriously, you celebrated your every birthday in an orphanage?" she said with her brows furrowed in what I assumed was disgust. I had no idea what they were discussing, but her reaction made me curious to eavesdrop.

"Well! We just shared our happiness, and also gifts and sweets with those poor kids," the boy said.

"And made them poorer?" she asked. I scowled, as I didn't get what she was trying to prove. I could have moved, but I wanted to know her point.

"Ever wondered what those kids crave for the most?" she asked next.

"Umm… I guess a better lifestyle, good food to eat and lots of toys,"

"Such a materialistic thought! No doubt you are born rich," she spurted a laugh laced with anger.

"And you are not?"

"You don't know me, Akhil,"

"Hey, my name is Akul,"

"Yeah, whatever. Well! They crave for affection, respect and acceptance. You guys go there and then cut a huge cake with lots of hugs and kisses from your parents. Then you show them how God blessed you with loving families, and not them! You show them how lavishly you celebrate your birthday! When many of them don't even know when they were born. Ever thought how badly that would have hurt them to realize that they have no one to make their day special?"

"Oh! Now you are getting emotional. Leave it. I was just trying to impress you. Let's talk about something else," the boy said, crushing the cigarette with his feet. I left the conversation as my phone again started buzzing in my hand. I pondered on their discussion, it was something I had never thought about. Even I used to celebrate the birthdays in an orphanage.

Shaking my head, I entered the hall and took in the panorama. The hall was colossal to hold this big event. At the right side, the dinner was arranged while the DJ had occupied the other side where people were dancing like crazy. I craned my neck to look for my friends and found them sitting on the table at the far end. I padded towards them. I noticed no one looked at me except Ekta as I advanced, even though they had sensed me approaching. Pulling the seat awkwardly when I was about to sit, Shaunik rose up to leave the table at the same instant. I felt my heart thumping with ire at his gesture. I pushed the seat back and turned to leave. I heard Ekta calling my name from behind, but I was done. I pulled my phone out and messaged my PA to fix the meeting with the Director of the publishing house regarding Partnership. This was another venture my father had started but couldn't make it happen. With this collaboration, we were going to enter in the children's books publishing under our brand name *TingTong*. I was stalling this meeting for a long time, as I wasn't sure if I was ready to pursue this idea. But now with a strong urge not to stay here anymore, I took this opportunity to sneak out from this place.

Blinded with rage and hurt, I jostled mindlessly through the crowd to get inside my room as fast as possible. I had had enough for the day. The next thing I knew was my collision with someone that resulted in the splash of a drink all over my face and shirt. Before I could react, I heard her voice again.

"Oh, God! Not again. Are you doing it deliberately? To get my attention? Let me make it clear then; I am not interested. And if it's not purposely, then you seriously need to learn to keep your eyes forward while walking," she said, dramatically shaking the splashed drink from her clothes, while still holding the glass of leftover drink in her other hand which looked like coke but I could undoubtedly assure from the pungent whiff, it was a cocktail drink. I looked dubiously at her, and her eyes widened in response.

"Don't you dare to blame me again. It wasn't my fault this time, neither the last time," she said, and I noticed the way her voice slurred. She was drunk without a shadow of a doubt.

She wore a short glittery black top with fitted blue denim. Her face caked with a layer of makeup. Her eyes tinted with kajal making them look big and mysterious. Her lips perfectly contoured with the red shade. Her hair tied on the top of her head in a chignon. Her fake eyelashes fluttered as she looked at me indignantly. I took an instant dislike to her appearance. I was more into natural looks rather than the made-up ones. Not interested in any further discussion, I ended the conversation with an apology.

"I am sorry," I said no longer feeling bad for my earlier rude behavior. She waved her hand, dismissing me and dashed towards the dance floor. She gulped the leftover drink without a flinch and started grooving on the music, throwing her hands up in the air, which made her short top rising further up, revealing her bare waist. I craned my neck to look at the crowd, and as expected, I wasn't the only one to ogle at her. She kept frolicking and swaying her body in rhythm with the beats without caring about the world. I didn't know her, but one thing was sure, she was the testimony of an over-pampered spoilt child. Perhaps her parents had spent more money on her than time.

I am no one to judge her. I told myself as I shook her thoughts out of my head. I rushed to my room and made-up my mind, to leave early morning the next day for the meeting. I decided not to inform Ekta, as she would try to stop me. I turned my phone silent and tossed it on the side table in my room. Pulling T-shirt over my head, I headed to th : bathroom for my night routine. As I slumped on my bed and slipped under the sheets, I promised myself to make the next day better.

CHAPTER 4

Down The Memory Lane

I glanced at my watch as I revved the engine of my car. It was half-past eight in the morning. I knew it was early, but this was the best time to sneak out without getting noticed, as everyone was busy preparing for the Haldi ceremony. Otherwise, I was sure Ekta would never let me leave without an argument that I could have never won. I was better at explaining my reasons over the phone than face to face. I was about to hit the accelerator of my car when I saw a female figure approaching me through the side mirror. She waved her hand to stop me. I slid down my window as she knocked on it.

"Oh! It's you!" she said with a scowl on her face as if she was expecting someone else. Why was she trying to stop me if she wasn't even sure who was inside the car? But I didn't tell her that. I just gave her a look that said it all.

"So your name is Ady, right?" she asked. If she thought that I was up for the chitchat to while away her time, then she was damn wrong. I was so exasperated that moment, I didn't care if I was rude to her again.

"Are you deliberately doing this? To get my attention? See, If you are looking for a toy to fritter away your morning boredom, let me make it clear, I am not interested," I said taking off my spectacles and cleaning them with my handkerchief. I liked the way my remark left her mouth agape.

"Great! So my foot is my tutor now," she said, rolling her eyes. I didn't know why, but her remark made me laugh, but that didn't mean she had gotten me.

"So Ady..." she started to say something, but I stopped her in the middle.

"I am Ady only for people who know me. You may call me Adyant Lohani," I replied.

"Okay, Adyant Lohani. Well! I am Riya! Just Riya and everyone calls me Riya. My name is not reserved yet," she said, lifting her hand for the shake. She drew it back when I didn't take it.

"May I know where are you going?" she asked.

"May I ask you why am I getting interviewed here?" I answered her question with another question, this time looking at her.

"Of course, Esha just told me that you are going to Delhi. Can I come with you? I have some urgent work there," she said, bobbing her head.

"Can you be a little bit more specific about the work?" I asked.

"Shopping. I need to go there for shopping," she replied, and I couldn't help the eye-roll.

Typical. Isn't it!

"See, I am in a hurry. You may ask someone else," I said, giving her my full attention now. I took in her appearance and realized that she looked different from yesterday. Maybe because there was no makeup on her face, her hair loose with wild waves and her eyes still had slight smudge kohl around them. She looked younger. More like a teenager, and perhaps she was. The thought made me a bit considerate towards her. But when I took in her attire, the same coarseness was back in a jiffy. The girl needed to learn to dress decently. She wore the shortest shorts I had ever seen with a sheer loose white top whose neck was so broad that it kept falling off her shoulder.

"Please…" she stretched the word *please* batting her eyes.

"No," I said, looking forward.

"Why?" she asked. I didn't care to reply and accelerated my car forward. I noticed my phone ringing and winced when I saw the caller ID. It was Esha. I stopped the car and took her call.

"Bhaiya, please, please, please, take her with you. At least my one day at the wedding will go without taunts,"

"I can't, Esha. I have an official meeting, and I don't have time for all this."

"She has never been to Delhi before. Leave her near any market on the way. She wouldn't know. You don't need to bother about her,"

"And what if I lost her?"

"That's even better. I want her gone anyway,"

"I don't think it's a good idea. You may ask someone else. I am pretty sure you will get many going to that side,"

"Do you want me to tell Ekta di that you are sneaking out? If not, then take her with you," she threatened me.

I huffed a sigh and craned my neck to look at the girl standing behind my car— *Riya*. She was still waiting there looking hopefully at my side. I flexed my fingers to call her and saw her jogging towards me.

"You have ten minutes. Go back and dress decently," I said as she stood near me.

"Excuse me?" she said with her hands on her hips.

"You heard me," I said without looking at her. I noticed her struggling to argue from the corner of my eye as she opened then closed her mouth but didn't say anything.

"Ten minutes," I said again, showing her my watch. She pivoted to run into the house again, leaving me there frustrated.

I tuned the FM on as I waited for her. I hummed the song as the radio station played Euphoria's *Maaeri*. A knock at the passenger side window made me aware of her arrival, and I unlocked the door for her. Sliding inside the car, she tapped on her wristwatch.

"I am here a minute before," she panted, as she made herself comfortable on the seat. She wore the same jeans that she had on the previous day with an oversized pale blue shirt.

"What?" she exclaimed as she caught me gawking at her. I shook my head as I turned the key to start the ignition.

"Had to borrow this shirt from a boy staying in the room next to me. I couldn't find anything 'decent' in my wardrobe," she stressed the word 'decent' and then rolled her eyes. I revved up the car, and she jerked a bit backward. She tilted on her seat to pull the seat belt and secured it in the buckle. Since we had started the journey, I felt her throwing incessant glares at me. I stole a glance at her side to confirm the doubt and found her tilted in my direction, still staring at me. And then this was my turn to question her, "What?"

"Are you always this rude with everyone or I am someone special?" she asked, tapping her finger on her lower lip dramatically. When I didn't reply and kept my concentration on the road, she added smiling wryly, "I guess people here aren't used to meeting awesome personalities,"

"Wearing fewer clothes, flirting with almost every boy, drinking, smoking and living like a hippie. Is it a new definition of awesomeness?" My reply was curt and paired with a quick glare. I knew that my words were crass, but I didn't care.

"Did I flirt with you?" she asked.

"What?" I asked, confused.

"Did I flirt with you?" she repeated pausing after every word.

"No,"

"Then what made you think so? It's wrong to judge people without knowing them, Adyant Lohani. Maybe I am just polite with the people who are kind to me, and if it looks like flirting, then let it be. I really don't care. And about my clothes and my eating/drinking habits, what I put on me or inside me is entirely my choice. That's nobody else's business," she said and turned on her seat to look straight at the road. I instantly felt terrible. I wanted to apologize but didn't.

"My bad. I presumed people here would be cool and forward. I didn't expect them to be an old fogey! Never mind! You know, I am used to these kinds of remarks, so it doesn't bother me," she added although, her reaction said quite the opposite. I nodded in response, kicking myself mentally for getting into this conversation with her. I decided to keep my mouth shut for the rest of the journey. Though the decision was short-lived because it wasn't mutual.

"What do you do, Adyant Lohani?" she asked, looking again at me. Her voice and question were decent enough to be answered.

"Call me, Adyant,"

"Aha! Does that mean I am going to get the privilege to be in your friend list soon? Who knows, maybe next you tell me to call you just Ady," she said mockingly, and I pretended to glare at her biting the back of my cheek to stifle my smile.

"Sorry," she said, holding her hands up. She cleared her throat and asked again, "So what do you do?"

"Freshly graduated. Running my father's business. Nothing fancy," I answered. I was no longer excited to talk about my profession, so I kept my answer to the point.

"Great. What kind of business?"

"We have a toy factory called *TingTong*,"

"Oh my god! Really? You know my younger brother had this *TingTong* sports car collection, and he was so obsessed with it," she said, and I couldn't help smiling at the praise. So I was wrong, and I did feel my chest swelling with the pride. I looked at her and found her looking down, engrossed in her reminiscences.

"He never let anyone touch them! Not even me! Can you imagine? He loved me more than anyone else but his *TingTong* cars," she added, looking up at me with a massive grin on her face. Her eyes were bright, and there was an enthusiasm in her voice as she talked about her brother. "I miss him so much," she added and looked wistful all of a sudden. I nodded barring myself from asking her any further questions about her and her family. She didn't speak for another few minutes and kept looking outside through the car window. I figured she loved her brother, but what made her look so melancholic, I couldn't understand.

"Did you have breakfast?" she asked after a while, and I shook my head in response.

"I am hungry. Can you stop somewhere so that I may grab something to munch… for both of us?"

"I have an urgent meeting at my office, and I am already running late. Mind if I head straight to my office? I will get the breakfast arranged for you there," I said without glancing at her direction.

"And what about shopping?"

"It's too early. Shops don't open before eleven. So you will have to wait till then,"

"Okay. Will you take me shopping then?"

"No. I will arrange the vehicle for you to shop and then drop you back at the farmhouse."

"You aren't coming back there with me?"

"It's uncertain," I answered when I was sure, I wasn't going back there. She nodded once and started looking outside the window. The next few minutes passed in silence as we weaved in and out of the morning traffic. It gave me time to contemplate my current condition. By the time I was around my office, I was confident that my decision was sensible and logical.

I stopped car outside a five-story building of *TingTong* in Delhi. I looked at Riya and found her in sound sleep with her head rested on the window.

"Riya, we are here," I shook her shoulder slightly to wake her up. She opened her eyes and looked here and there disoriented.

"We are here," I explained, seeing her confused. I clambered off the car and rounded the car to open the door for her. As we entered the building, a receptionist sitting at the desk right in front of the main entrance, greeted both of us.

"Your appointment for today morning has arrived, and Mrs Singh has already started the meeting," she informed me as she led me to the boardroom. I stopped at my cabin and opened the door for Riya.

"You may wait here, meanwhile. Your breakfast will be here soon," I said and then turned towards the receptionist, "Can you make the arrangements for the breakfast?"

"Can I have a pizza? One with olives and baby corn topping?" Riya chimed in, and we both looked at her astonished.

"Pizza for breakfast?" I asked arching my brow at her. Scrunching her nose, she replied, "I know, it's a bit costly, but don't worry I am paying for it," she patted her purse to indicate she had got the money.

"That wasn't what I mean," I said and then turned my face towards the receptionist, "Can you order a Pizza for her?"

"Certainly sir," she replied, trying to stifle her smile. Leaving Riya there, I headed towards the boardroom. I opened the door and found five people sitting around the table.

"Here he is," Mrs Singh, my manager of the Delhi branch, rose from her seat and walked towards me. Patting my back, she introduced me to the members, "He is Mr Adyant Lohani, CEO of *TingTong*. And I must say he is very talented. The way he has taken over his father's industry is commendable,"

I knew she was exaggerating, but I didn't correct her. It seemed like just yesterday when my life turned upside down. I had just taken over the business; I knew nothing about it. I had no interest in it, as my whole focus was on the music, and my father never even tried to push me into it. But the future is unseen, and the unexpected happened. Now I was getting acquainted with the industry under Mrs Singh's guidance. She had been working with my father since he opened a branch in Delhi.

Time blurred as we sat down and started discussing the terms and conditions for collaboration. In the next hour, we discussed the strategies for our new venture in the publishing, and by the end of the meeting, everyone came to a consensus with the terms. We gave them full rights where publishing was concerned but kept the branding and marketing under *TingTong*. The meeting had taken more time than I had intended to devote, but I was happy with the outcome. My dad was so eager for this venture. He always had a soft corner for literature, and seeing kids preferring electronic gadgets and toys over the books had made him keener to add books to the *TingTong*. His vision was to make every kid experience the fantasy world that books create because the wisdom one attains from the experiences of imaginary characters is more persuasive, which always stays with you. I bade my farewell to the members and marched back to my cabin. As I walked through the corridor, I opened my phone and found numerous missed calls from Ekta. I was still glancing at the screen when my phone again buzzed displaying her number on the screen. I took the call preparing myself to explain.

"Hey,"

"Why aren't you here, Ady?" she asked, ignoring my pleasantries.

"Umm… I had a meeting today. It was urgent," I tried to explain.

"Yesterday, when I asked you about your schedule, it wasn't there. Was it?" her voice was uptight that told me she wasn't going to buy any of my excuses. So I decided to be honest with her.

"Look, Ekta, I don't think I want to be there—" but before I could complete, she shut me up in the middle.

"Why, Ady? Why it's always about you? You want it then you don't want it. Why you can't do something because I want it. It's my day, Ady, and I want you here. So unless the reason is you can't see me marrying someone else, I want you to get your ass back here. And it's not a request." She completed in her trembling voice, making me completely speechless.

"I am coming back," I replied, not wanting to hurt her anymore. She had always supported me like a true friend—and though unintentionally I had become that thorn in her feet that wouldn't allow her to move forward even if she wanted to.

"Good!" she said and ended the call.

CHAPTER 5

Down The Memory Lane

After talking to Ekta and kicking myself mentally for behaving like a child, I strolled towards my cabin. As I opened the door, a smile crept on my face. Riya was standing at the far end of my office, facing the glass window. My guitar in her hand as she randomly strummed the chords. She was singing a song in her gravelly voice that was entirely out of sync with the music. Even the lyrics of the song were wrong, yet her attempt seemed honest. Any kind of music is right if it makes you enjoy the moment. She was so engrossed in it that she didn't even notice me entering the room. She kept on singing and pretending like a rock star that is singing for the audience. She occasionally threw her head back on the higher notes, which were entirely inharmonious. I wanted to watch her charade a bit more, but the musician in me couldn't handle the out of sync notes, so I started singing the stanza to correct her. She immediately pivoted and looked at me, stunned. It was rewarding to see her speechless for a moment.

I kept on completing the song as she ascended in my direction. Once she was just a foot distance away from me, she offered me the guitar that was in her hand. I took it merrily and started strumming the chords in rhythm with the lyrics. I moved and leaned my back on the desk facing her. Closing my eyes, I sang in high and clear falsetto. The whole tension, anger, and doubts seemed to alleviate with every exhale of my breath. And as I finished the song, I felt high-spirited. I opened my eyes and saw her smiling ear to ear. She made a soundless clap to applaud.

"Wow… It's a tough song, and you sang it so effortlessly. Even better than I sang it," she said, and I snickered.

"Well! Thank you. I am overwhelmed by your praise," I said, keeping the guitar on the desk.

"Hey, sing some more for me," she exclaimed.

"No. It's time to go. We have to head back before the evening," I said.

"You are coming with me?" she asked, narrowing her eyes.

"Yes. I am,"

"That's great. I need help in selecting a dress for me," she said.

"A dress? You bothered to come so far just for a dress?" I said, shaking my head.

"Hmm… I came to the wedding unprepared. I don't have anything to wear that seems 'appropriate' for this occasion," she air quoted the 'appropriate'. "Moreover, I am tired of people ogling at me and making uncouth remarks. It's been ages since I bought something traditional for myself. I am not into these Indian dresses," she said, scrunching her nose as if she loathed traditional wears. I nodded without saying anything, and the easiness I had just gained with her was gone. Call me a fogyish, but that's how I was. We walked out in silence as I ticked the options in my head where I could take her for the shopping. Connaught place seemed the nearest and most appropriate.

"You are an amazing singer. You should think about changing your profession," she said as we slid inside the car. Did she realize she just rubbed salt into my wounds? I glanced at her; she seemed genuine.

"That's a lost dream now," I replied nonchalantly.

"Why? No dream is a lost dream if you are still alive," she said as she fastened the seat belt.

"It's a long story," I replied, clearly indicating that I wasn't interested in the conversation.

"Oh! Meanwhile, you didn't comment on my singing," she said with tongue in cheek.

"Was that singing? Have you ever been told that you are a terrible singer?" I replied, now smiling reminiscing the scene in my office.

"Many times, but I don't give a damn. I sing for myself, and I love my singing—and you know what? Before I get old, I am going to record an album in my voice so that I can hear it when I have no teeth left in my mouth," she replied.

"Full of yourself, aren't you?" I said, smiling, and she shrugged in response.

Next few minutes flew away talking about everything and nothing. She kept asking me about the Delhi streets, and I answered as we weaved through the traffic to reach Connaught Place. I parked the car at the parking and steered her to the way towards a shop that had traditional wears displayed outside. I had noticed it on the road. She was walking a few steps behind me when I heard her cursing someone. When I looked back, I realized that all those swearing were aimed at me. Her cheeks were red because of the sweltering hot wind.

"What's wrong?" I asked, seeing her scowling at me.

"It's too hot, and just because of some stupid guy, I am wearing too many clothes," she carped. I looked at her up and down and then at myself. "There is nothing to complain as you are wearing as many layers as I am," I said.

"But I am not comfortable," she whined.

"Comfortable? Really? Don't tell me you feel comfortable in those tight-fitting and skin-revealing clothes with almost everyone ogling at you. And not in a decent way," I countered folding my arms. It was incredible to see her reaction. Mouth agape but nothing came out of it. "Now, here is the shop—" I said beckoning towards the shop "—I guess you will get here whatever you want,"

"Fuddy-duddy," she murmured.

"What?"

"Nothing. And what about you?" she asked.

"I will be waiting in the car," I took out my visiting card from my wallet and handed it over to her before adding, "My mobile number is there. You may call me once your shopping is over." She took the card from me and studied it for a few seconds.

"Does that mean you are going to leave me here alone?" she asked, and I gave her a look in return that screamed '*obviously, what else are you expecting.*'

"No way! With such an old-school thinking, how can you leave a girl alone in this cruel and big city?" she said, batting her eyes, and I narrowed my eyes in response. "This is the first time I am here. What if someone fooled and looted me. Oh my god! What if I get kidnapped?" she said dramatically placing her hand on her chest as if she was scared to even think about that scenario.

"There is no need to overreact. I am just a street away,"

"Okay, but I am telling you, if anything happens to me, you will be responsible," she said, and I had to pinch the bridge of my nose to maintain the composure.

"Okay, I am coming with you, but please make it quick. I hate shopping," I said as I followed her to the shop.

"Why do you hate it? Don't you have a girlfriend?" she turned to face me and walked backwards.

"No," I replied, and her lips formed O as if she was stunned.

"Walk properly, Riya, you will fall," I warned her.

"You don't have now, or you never had?" she asked, snubbing my warning. I didn't know what made her so surprised. It wasn't mandatory to have a girlfriend. Or was it?

"Never had," I replied and saw her eyes widening.

"How may I help you?" A loud voice made her jump as the salesman appeared suddenly behind her, saving me from any further interrogation.

"Is this how you welcome the customers here? You scared the shit out of me," she rebuked, and salesman appeared embarrassed. Shaking her head, Riya explained to him what she wanted. I looked around and found a statue wearing an off-white saree embellished with golden sequin. I didn't know why I felt like this was the right dress for her. And next, I found myself voicing my opinion.

"This one is stunning. I think this will look good on you," she pivoted instantly to look at me first and then towards the statue. She observed it, and I could see the admiration on her face. She moved a bit closer to check the quality of cloth first and then she turned the price tag stapled on it. Her eyebrows shoot up at the five-digit figure. She took a step back and said, "I don't know how to wear a saree. And I don't think anyone there will be happy to help me."

"That's no problem, ma'am, we can get it stitched, then you can wear it just like a skirt," the salesman elucidated, but she shook her head in response.

"I will like to see some more designs," she said.

Was the price a problem? She seemed to like it, yet she didn't give it a second glance. A thought appeared from nowhere, which couldn't be right, because, by her manner of living, she seemed to belong to an affluent family. Money couldn't be the hitch then why did her demeanour change after seeing the price tag? Before I could stop myself, my hand flew to her elbow as I stopped her from heading further inside the store.

"What's the problem with this one?" I asked out of curiosity. She raised herself slightly to whisper in my ear, "You shouldn't buy the first thing you see in the store. It's the rule of shopping,"

"Really? And who made this rule?"

"A great shopping connoisseur. And that's me. Now follow me," she started to walk beckoning me to follow her. An hour blurred, as she rifled through almost everything in the store.

"I think I will go with that first saree," she said, looking at my annoyed face and then at the statue wearing the saree that I had suggested her first.

"What happened to the great advice of the great connoisseur?" I asked with a sarcastic quirk of my brow.

"She also told to break the rule if the people around you start to lose their minds," she said, darting her gaze between salesman and me who also seemed as frustrated as I was.

"Are you sure you can make it easy to wear?" she asked the salesman.

"Don't worry Ma'am. It will be as easy as wearing a scarf," he said, taking out another piece of the saree that Riya had selected.

"How much time it's going to take for stitching?" I asked.

"One to two hours," he replied, heading towards the billing counter. The good boy that I was, I opened my wallet to pay for the article, but Riya stopped me narrowing her eyes.

"What do you think you are doing? Who do you think you are? Are you my husband or boyfriend or a relative? I don't take favours from strangers," she said, opening her purse and taking out the credit card. Should I make her realize that she came all-alone with the same stranger? But I didn't poke her with the jibe. She closed her eyes shut momentarily as the cashier swiped the card and murmured, "Someone is going to lose his shit today." She took the bill and after a while tailor took her measurements. A few minutes later, when we were outside the shop, my gaze fell on a street toy vendor selling the Helicopters. I smiled reminiscing my childhood. Riya might have noticed me smiling because just after that, she hurled a question at me.

"Now what's so amusing about the Helicopter?" she asked, and I pursed my lips as my smile widened.

"As a child, I was so fascinated with the Helicopters that my father had to add the helicopters to his product line. It was the first mechanical toy by *TingTong*, earlier we were just into the soft toys," I replied and smiled wistfully realizing my father was no longer with me to go to any extent to fulfil my wishes.

"You know what I was fascinated with as a child?" she said, looking blankly ahead. I looked at her as she continued without waiting for my reply. "A doll," she said and then looked at me. "Clichéd, isn't it?" she added, crunching her nose. "But what clichéd wasn't that I never got one," she laughed humorlessly.

"Why?" I asked, and she just shrugged in response without looking at me. I did notice the way her shoulders slumped, and eyes froze ahead blankly. Something in her gesture told me that the confidence she exuded was tinged with something, I couldn't figure out. And before I could fathom, she recovered and straightened her back.

"What's next?" the sudden change in the topic and her demeanor didn't get unnoticed, but I didn't prod either. She rummaged through her bag as her phone started ringing. I didn't know who it was, but the scowl on her face told me it wasn't one of her favorites. She ignored the call and tossed the phone inside her bag after silencing it. She looked at me with the arched brow for the answer and then I remembered she had asked something.

"We may wait in a nearby restaurant—" she didn't let me complete and chimed in, "Not restaurant. I would rather prefer Dilli ki Garam Hawa. Show me around. At least I will get to tick off Delhi from my bucket list."

"It's too hot to roam around at this time of the month, and we don't even have much time," I reasoned.

"Okay, then choose something nearby," she said resolutely with her chin up. A white spaghetti top peeped out as she unbuttoned her shirt, removed it and tied it around her waist.

"Don't take it off. It's too sunny. You will get tan," I said, looking at her now exposed skin.

"And I love to get tan. You know tanned bodies are a sign that someone has actually lived his or her life," she said, gathering all the curly tendrils and bringing them up together to tie them in a bun on the top of her head. A few shiny locks escaped and framed her heart-shaped face. With a quick swipe of her fingers, she tucked them behind her ears. Her attention was diverted as her phone again started ringing. She muttered a curse before taking the call indignantly.

"Yes," she said to someone on the phone. I couldn't hear what the other person was talking about, but her gestures showed me she was irritated.

"Hmm… I did," she said, rolling her eyes at something the person was speaking on the other end.

"Yeah? Is the amount too much? Trust me it's nothing as compared to what your wife spends on her shoes," she said and then I realized it might be regarding her latest purchase.

"Okay, that's no problem. Let me call *Nana* regarding this," she said, and her smile turned wicked at something the other person had said.

"Ah! Now you are talking. You are so sweet. Love you, Dad," she said sarcastically. Clicking the call end, she threw her phone inside her bag. From her conversation, I conjectured that she had a tainted relationship with her parents.

"So?" she said, quirking her brow.

"Umm… How about *Agrasen Ki Baoli*? It's a monument. I haven't been there myself, but I have heard that place is a retreat in scorching summers," I said.

"Then take me there," she said, snaking her hand around my arm. In any other scenario, I would have found it awkward, but I didn't feel that way with her arm laced around mine. Did that mean I had started to like her? *No way!*

"What else is there in your bucket list?" I asked as we started walking.

"It's very long. Mainly includes the oceans, deserts and mountains," Riya said, counting three on her fingers.

"Why?"

"Because they make me endure all the pain," she said and then laughed on herself shaking her head. Though she hid it well, the first time I saw the glimpse of that vulnerable girl, which was quite the opposite of her tough exterior.

"Wow… that could be the lyrics of a song," I said, repeating those lines in my head.

"Oceans, deserts and mountains, make me endure all the pain," she said and smiled at me. "Do write a song about it when you become famous," she added, clasping her hand in mine.

"Yeah. So travelling is something you are passionate about. Is it?" I asked snubbing her earlier statement.

"Now speaking of passion reminds me that you are supposed to tell me your long story. We have more than an hour now, and I guess that would be more than enough," she said cleverly dodging what I had asked and turning the tables on me. I was in no mood to talk about my gloomy life. I was enjoying her carefree and blatant attitude. She was someone who knew nothing about my life and me, and I was looking forward to forgetting everything for some time, but her question threw me off-kilter. Dodging what she had asked me, I drew my hand out of her grip and started pacing faster, assuming that she would get the hint. But she was quick to tug at my hand, halting me all of a sudden.

"Don't run. And don't give up. You have got the real dream… and also the talent," she said, still holding my hand in hers. Something about the way she said those words made a shudder go through my spine. I looked at her flabbergasted. I had no idea what she was talking about, yet it seemed from her expressions that she was sure about what she had just said. She might have read the confusion etched on my face as she said, "I am sorry, but I overheard your conversation with your friends yesterday. And now as I know what an amazing singer you are, I am not letting such a talent go to waste," she said with utter seriousness that I had seen on her face for the first time since we met. *Great!* So I wasn't the only one to eavesdrop.

"Things aren't that simple, Riya. You don't know my situation. I know what I am doing," I replied, jerking my hand out of her grip.

"No! You don't. If you had known what you were doing, you would have stayed there and fought to prove your point to your friends rather than running. And things are never going to be simple, so it's better to at least keep your response simple," and suddenly she was talking like all grown up and mature as if she had seen the world, and on the other hand,

I was a petulant child that needed counselling. I pivoted and strode ahead. She had to run to be on my heel, but I didn't care.

"Adyant, stop and listen. Please," she said. I stopped and spun to hurl the rage out on her. The words were off my tongue before I could filter them.

"Mind your own business! It would be better if you concentrate on your life rather than meddling in others. Do you even have any idea what people think about you? How do they talk about you behind your back? The names they call you by?" A disappointed look clouded her face instantly, and to brush it off, she ducked her head before she thought I noticed it. I immediately felt bad, but I was too adamant for apologizing at that moment. She nodded and then looked up at me, veiling the hurt under a bright smile. I turned and started walking away from her. Perhaps she was right. I preferred to run rather than fighting. She followed me but remained a step behind. After a few minutes, we were inside the Agarsen ki baoli. The place wasn't crowded. We directly went down the steps. The relief coursed through the body as I experienced a drop in the temperature, and the relaxed exhale from her told me that she too felt the same.

I gestured her to sit down, and she complied, but she chose to sit a step ahead of me. She didn't look back at me and neither she tried to talk to me. I laced my fingers together before the apologies spurted out of my mouth.

"I am sorry. I shouldn't have said that,"

"Why men have to be so irrational sometimes?" she said, and then shook her head as if she disapproved what she just said. "Most of the time. No. All the time," she corrected, and I stifled my laugh.

"I said I am sorry," I repeated.

"It's fine. Anyway, it wasn't the first time someone had said that to me," without looking back at me she picked up a stone and started drawing the random shapes on the step.

"Don't you feel bad… or angry?" I asked. I wanted to know why she wasn't affected by all the uncouth remarks if she was aware of them. She never seemed to care about what people thought or talked about her.

"No. I don't feel bad or angry. Rather I feel pity. They are the people with their thoughts bounded to the societal norms. They don't even know what freedom is! How it feels to fly high in the sky without your feet shackled to the ground! They are captive of their own fears. They have made prisons of themselves, and they think it's the right way of living. They can't digest that there is life beyond those bars, and they try to chain if someone tries to break those bars. I am a free bird. Nothing can hold me back, that's why they chose to bitch about me, and because that's the only thing they can do. I am master of my own desires and dreams, and I don't give a fuck what they think about me," she said haughtily, and I smiled at her narcissism.

"Enough about me! Now tell me your story," she said out of nowhere.

"Which story?" I feigned to think.

"Lost dream, singer,"

"Why should I tell you? Give me one reason," I said, pressing my lips in a thin line.

"One, you will feel better. And may lose the chip you are carrying on your shoulder. Two, I am no one to you, so I won't judge you for your choices. Three, sometimes all it takes is saying it aloud, so that you may figure out the next step. You need more reasons?"

"No. It's enough. And the chip on my shoulder, eh?" I said mockingly, and she laughed.

"Now, spill it out," she said, turning in her seat to look at me.

"Well! I, with my friends, was supposed to start this music band. Our families supported us until life ditched me, and I ditched my friends. My father suffered a stroke and died. I had to look after his business, so I gave up on dream that we had seen together. Now my friends are angry and hurt," I said, looking straight towards the descending stairs.

"That's not a long story," she said, and I smiled.

"Why did you choose business over singing? Is it something you are more passionate about?"

"No. But sometimes you have to think beyond yourself. There are a lot of people who work for this industry, and hence they depend on me, and so their families. Moreover, there is not much scope in doing anything in art. The other career options can get you an assured life, while things will always be uncertain if I pursue a career in singing. Not everyone can be a Rock star," I repeated the lines I had been hearing from my relatives and family.

"You are right, sometimes art can't get you luxuries, but it gives you something bigger than that. That's called satisfaction. It may not give you a comfy bed, but a sound sleep is assured." I had no answer to that because I knew she was right, so I just nodded.

"Why can't you handle both the things together?" she asl ed.

"Because these two things are entirely different, and demand a lot of time. Running both of them together will be like sailing in two boats and eventually capsizing both,"

"That's just your presumption; it may not be necessary. How can you say that without trying? And it's not difficult either; all you need to do is divide your time skillfully," she said.

"Actually unlike some geniuses like you, normal people have just twenty-four hours in a day," I said sarcastically.

"True. Normal people have twenty-four hours in a day, but people with a dream have one thousand four hundred and forty minutes a day. And people with passion and determination have eighty-six thousand four hundred seconds in a day. So these are just excuses. Admit that you are not passionate enough," she said with a smirk on her face as she wiggled her brows at me. Her words did hit the target and pulled at so many things deep within me, making me feel like a wounded animal ready to attack. I had a sudden urge to wipe off that look from her face with another jibe, and like a jerk I had been to her earlier, I did the same again.

I laughed with exasperation in my voice. Resting my palms on the back step, I supported my weight on them. "It's so easy to say. Isn't it? That too when all you have to worry about is which dress to wear and what lipstick to match. Tell me something about your dreams. What are you passionate about, Riya?" Amped up with the rage, I refuted her because I didn't want to agree with her logic. I didn't want to crumble the safety walls I had unintentionally created around me, because outside it, lied the challenges I wasn't ready to face. I deliberately chose my words to shut her up. I wasn't behaving like me. I didn't know why, but I was different with her. One moment considerate and another moment ready to hurt her, but unlike me, her voice was polite when she answered.

"You know when God decided to give life, he never intended to make it easy. It was supposed to be difficult, and that's why he blessed us with the brain. It's sad that most people lose it when they require it the most," she looked at me and narrowed her eyes, and I got the hint that the insult was aimed at me.

"No matter how well off or poor or intelligent or stupid you are, everyone has to face complications at some point in their lives. And you can't compare one life to another to satisfy your insecurities. And regarding my dreams, I do have, but their fruition is not in my hands," she added, and with that, all her philosophies got drained in the trench. It's always easy to give suggestions to others but difficult and nearly impossible when they have to implement them in their own life.

"So are you saying you are not passionate enough?" I asked mockingly.

"I am just saying it's not in my hands," her tone was curt, and I decided not to prod her further, but perhaps my expressions might have given her the hints about my thoughts.

"You are bent on proving me wrong. Aren't you? But you have no idea how stubborn I am. And moreover, we aren't talking about me here, because it's not me who is wandering here and there mindlessly, bumping into random people and then lashing out all the anger on them," she carped holding up her hand to show me the impression of her smudged mehndi and I couldn't help the smile that curved my lips.

"I am sorry,"

"You should be. You were rude,"

"I know," I said, pursing my lips in a thin line.

"So, are you going to give it a try? Because if you want it bad enough, you will make it happen anyhow. And if not, you will look for excuses. Now contemplate what you are actually doing!" she talked like as if she had experienced everything in life.

"How old are you?"

"Excuse me?" she exclaimed at my irrelevant interrogation.

"You talk like as if you have seen much more life as compared to me. Do you actually know what the real difficulties are? You talk about big things, but your well-manicured hands are telling a different story altogether. Can you tell me something about your achievements? I want to know how you have implemented all these theories in your life." I knew I was being a total jerk while she had been trying to push me towards my goal.

"You think one has to be aged to gain experience in life? That's the most-immature thought, Mr Lohani. And about my achievements, well! I have achieved life… on my terms. Now beat that," she said, looking snootily at me, and all I could do was admire her confidence. Despite my numerous efforts to humiliate her, she shone brighter with her every retort.

"Whatever you are saying is correct, and I appreciate your thoughts, but life isn't a bed of roses for everyone," I said.

"I can't agree more, but most of the times, these difficulties are only in our head," she paused for a moment, and I looked at her waiting for her to complete. She gazed blankly at the stairs, and after a hiatus, she added, "One stressful day at the office and people forget to cherish the hugs and kisses of their kids that they get on arriving at home and don't think twice before calling it a bad day. See, they let a lousy moment devour all the happy moments in a day.

"A break up with girlfriend or boyfriend and people forget the selfless love of their parents and don't think twice before calling true love an illusion. See, they let a bad experienced poisoned the heart that was filled with love before.

"A rejection at a job interview and people forget that the rejected candidates are way more than the selected ones and don't think twice before cursing their fate. Life is never a bed of roses, but most of the time; it's us who put the thorns in it with our negative attitude.

"Your situation is just the same. You have got everything—the talent, the money and the team, yet you are focusing on the minute obstacles," she said, and I felt completely stripped to the bones. Was it actually what I was doing? Was I really not passionate enough? Was that the reason my friends were so offended? I was surprised how effortlessly she made me question my own intentions. Despite the turmoil she had created in my head, I was adamant not to admit it in front of her.

"Big talks," I said, shaking my head and laughing mockingly. I turned in her direction and looked at her. Giving her my full attention, I challenged her, "Tell me about the difficulties that you have faced in your life. Just a single but a genuine one, and I promise I will give my singing a shot, even if I have to give up on my father's business," I said. I didn't know if I was challenging her or myself. Despite the defiant look on my face, she smiled. Lifting her hand, she crooked her little finger and said, "Pinky promise?"

And like an idiot, I laced my pinky with hers. She kept her eyes locked with mine, and I could read the various emotions that clouded her face. I could sense the fight she was having inside, but soon she masked it with a teasing smile. She withdrew her hand and looked straight for a while. The coos of pigeons accompanied by screeches of bats replaced the silence between us.

"Where were you born, Adyant?" She broke the ice without looking at me.

"Umm… Dehradun," I answered, looking at the side of her face. Where was she going with that? I wondered.

"Wow… If I am not wrong, it must be one of the top class hospitals in Dehradun. Was it?" she glanced at my way this time.

"Yeah, it was,"

"Do you know where I was born?" she asked with a serious expression plastered on her face.

"Where?" I asked. I didn't know why I was holding my breath.

"I don't know," she replied and then laughed. I sighed and shook my head. I didn't know why I was expecting a thoughtful conversation with her.

"But I do know where I was found," she said gently with a smile still tugged on her lips. I was expecting another joke, but what she said next shook me to the core.

CHAPTER 6

Down The Memory Lane

"In a trash-bin outside a government hospital in Bijnaur. My parents… umm… someone had left me there to die just after a few minutes of my birth," she said and paused for a moment, leaving me covered in goosebumps.

Can it be true? It can't.

"Next day, when someone came to clear the trash bin, they found me there with my body covered in blue and red bruises. There were even a few glass pieces that had pierced my skin," she said, and I found myself shaken. I looked at her with my eyes wide open, while she kept looking towards the stairs blankly. It wasn't kind of thing that I hadn't heard of before, but hearing it from someone who had actually faced all this was a terrible experience. A voice in my head told me, not to believe what all she was saying. Maybe it was her another ruse to fool me. But what was her benefit in that? I came out of the trance as she continued, "I was admitted to the hospital immediately as I was still breathing, but there was no chance of the survival. Then the miracle happened, and I endured," she said, raising her hands in the gesture of self-appreciation.

"You know I also have a certificate from the same hospital for my remarkable survival," she said excitedly, turning towards me, but I was too numb to say anything.

"I was sent to an orphanage once my condition was stable—"

"How do you know all this?" I asked interrupting her. The hospital or the orphanage couldn't be that brutal to reveal all this to a child.

"A year ago, I had this sudden urge to find my real parents. When I started the search, I came across all this," she replied. Several queries started cramming my mind. Didn't she mention a younger brother on our way to here? Didn't she talk to her father after shopping? But before I could ask her, she started narrating again.

"I grew up in the orphanage until the age of twelve. It was a good time there. I had friends. Some of them got adopted. Some stayed with me. Some died too."

A gasp might have escaped from my lips as her eyes darted in my direction. When I didn't say anything, she averted her eyes and continued. "I was twelve when a beautiful doctor couple conducted a free health check-up camp in our orphanage. They were friendly and very kind. They did all the tests and gave free medicines to the one who had some problem for free. After two weeks they again came to the orphanage intending to adopt me. I still remember that day when they came to see me along with their four years old boy. I found them doting and caring. They had this big house in Kanpur. I got my separate room, my separate wardrobe and my study table," she looked wistful for a moment and then she was smiling again.

"Everything was great for the first few months. They pampered me, fed me a healthy diet, conducted many medical tests and gave me the medicines saying that I was deficient. One day they told me that my brother was sick, and I was the only one who could save his life. He was an adorable child. I would have done anything to save him. His kidneys were damaged, and I was the match. I donated my kidney to him, and his life was saved. Now, as their purpose was solved, I was of no use for them. They started treating me differently. They weren't as loving towards me as they were to their son. They both were busy people. My father—"

she laughed mockingly "—often came late from the hospital, whereas my mother had her clinic to run. One day I learnt from their conversation that they never adopted me out of love. That free health check-up camp was a pretence to find the match for their son's kidney transplantation. I was hurt, but my brother was the ultimate prize. He loved me, unconditionally. More than he loved his parents because they never had time for him. He used to sneak out from his parent's bedroom to sleep with me. I was supposed to look after him when they both worked. I was supposed to cook their breakfast and dinner. It was still ok. I had a better school to study in. I had a better bed to sleep and better food to eat. It was a win-win situation for both of us. But it did make me detached emotionally from them. Things were still going good," she paused for a moment and then exhaled loudly before continuing, "I was sixteen when my so-called father started looking at me in a way that made me uncomfortable. He started fondling me, and also bringing gifts for me. That too, without his wife's knowledge. As time passed, he began touching me inappropriately saying that I needed a body checkup.

"Once we both were alone at home. I was preparing for my pre-boards when he came to my room. Drunk. He hugged me from behind. The way his hand ran on my body made me feel so dirty that I attacked his hand with the compass. He threw me on the ground and cried in pain. Then he hit me back.

"He slapped me, kicked me, pulled my hair and also jabbed my hand with the same compass," she unintentionally rubbed her thumb on a scar on the backside of her right hand, that I assumed to be from the same incident she was narrating.

"Till the time his wife arrived, I was bruised red and blue. For the second time in sixteen years," she smiled sadly, and then her eyes twinkled as she added, "I think I was destined for cruel parents,"

I didn't realize that I had clenched my hands to the extent that my knuckles were turned white. My jaw was tight with the fury. How could someone do that to his daughter? For someone like me, who had gotten the best of both worlds, it was difficult to understand. I was blessed with loving parents, who were never rude to anyone, let alone abusing or beating their own child. She didn't say anything further, but I couldn't hold back my fervor, "Then? Did your mother support you?"

"No. He told her that he caught me red-handed stealing, and was teaching me a lesson. That day I realized that I was no one to them. They never considered me more than a body that could save their child and after that, a permanently adopted housemaid. She didn't even bother to hear my side of the story and threatened me to call the police. I don't know why, but I was scared. If I were who I am today, I would have called the police myself," she said smirking.

"That night was an eye-opener for me. I cried on my bed for the whole night, nursing my wounds and promising myself that this would be the last time I was crying. I had a realization that day that I can't just sit and wait for the opportunity to make my life better. My days weren't going to flip just with the twist of fate, because God had forgotten to write the one for me. And then it dawned on me, how lucky I was! He didn't write my fate because he wanted me to write it to myself. He had actually given the pen in my hand to write my own fate. When the things get upside down, it's God's way to tell us that the pen is in our hand now. I realized that I had to create opportunities for me and make my life better. I had survived before, and I would have survived then too, but this time, I wanted to live my life too."

"Then what did you do?"

"I talked to *Nana*," she said, and it reminded me that she had taken this name during her conversation with her bastard father.

"He was an infamous old lawyer. He used to be there at the park when I took my younger brother there for playing. Every kid in the park called him *Nana*. I don't know how, but he had sensed that something was wrong with me. He tried to talk to me several times, but I dodged him because of his reputation. After that night, I went to him, showed him my bruises and told him everything that had happened the other day, and also the things that happened before. He agreed to help me but needed a strong proof against my father so that he couldn't have any way out. He suggested me a trick. Though it was weird yet I agreed. He told me to abet my father and record everything. He gave me a Handycam and taught me how to use it. I did the same and succeeded, though it left me again bruised," she said with a triumphant on her face.

"And then you went to the police and filed the case. Is it?" I asked, keen to know if he got punished or not.

"No. We blackmailed him. *Nana* made a strong case against him, not only regarding the abuse but also for the adoption with unethical intention, but didn't file it. There was a reason he was infamous. According to him, with the money and power, my father would have either proved him guilty free or dragged the case for years. So he threatened him, and in return wanted him to make arrangements for me in one of the best boarding school and provide me with whatever I want," she nibbled her lower lip as the mischievous glint colored her face, "I still remember his face. I had never seen him so helpless. He was even ready to fall on my feet. He had to agree because his reputation and career were on stake. Everything changed after that. Life is all set now, as you can see," she smiled at me, and I returned her smile. "I wanted to pay Nana his fees, but he told me that I don't need to worry about it," she snickered. She looked content as if she had no regrets, no complaints. She peered at me and found me staring at her considerately.

"And before you ask, no, I don't feel selfish or guilty of what I did. That incident changed my perspective on life. People are selfish. Love is selfish. They won't love you unless they have some hidden motive behind it. Love for them is just the way to use people for their benefit. I learnt there is nothing bad in using people. God didn't bless me with a family. So I assume everyone who comes into my life has a purpose. I just make sure it's for my benefit. And I don't regret doing it. I am no longer a crybaby who keeps on blaming circumstances and other people. I learned to love myself more than anyone else," she said, her voice exuded the grit as if she was sure of what she was saying.

"My lifestyle may be inappropriate for many, but at least it makes them notice me. Earlier, no one was aware of my existence. This boldness, this attitude makes me look strong and acceptable. At least it screams that I am shrewd enough not to be fooled by anyone. It's me now who uses people and not the other way," she said as if justifying herself, but she didn't need to. I nodded in response, though. I understood it was her way to get the attention. I didn't know if she was right or wrong. I couldn't imagine myself in her shoe to judge her based on her choices. She had learnt something from her own experience, and I was no one to pass the verdict.

"Now does that count as difficult experience? Or shall I add more to it?" she asked, pulling me out of my reverie. I laughed softly and all of a sudden, I was seeing her in a new light. Everything she said or did that seemed inapt before appeared pertinent now. When her eyes met with mine, I saw something real behind those big brown eyes. The struggle, the hurt, the anger and much more of those sixteen years concealed behind the mask of a carefree and reckless girl. Sympathy engulfed me as I thought of a little girl she was once all by herself in this cruel world. My heart ached thinking that she never got to experience the comfort of a mother's lap, the strength of a father's arm, warm cuddles on the scary nights and a loving caress on tough days. Being a spectator of her misery, I felt responsible for her suffering.

I wished if I could have done anything to lessen her pain, which was not possible because I didn't know her then. What surprised me was despite that she felt the need show me the right path. She fought her own battle and if she could do it all alone, why couldn't I.

"Don't look at me that way," she broke my trance. "I hate when people look at me sympathetically," she added.

"How old are you now?" I asked.

"You aren't supposed to ask a lady her age," she told me mockingly.

"I guess someone just taught me to break all the societal norms," I said slyly, and she laughed.

"You are a fast learner. Well! I am nineteen, and you?" she said.

"Twenty-two," I replied.

"Are you going to keep your promise then?" she asked, arching her brows.

"It's going to be an uphill struggle," I sighed with my gaze fixed on hers. I fought the smile on my face as I earned a scoff and raise of brows from her—A clear indication that she was ready to argue more. But before she could come up with a retort, I added, "But Yes, I am going to keep the promise. After all, I have eighty-six thousand four hundred seconds in a day. I think I can make it happen," I winked at her. I was still unsure of how I was going to bring it to fruition. But I wasn't going to blow off the light she had just ignited in me.

"That's like a champ," she said and held up her hand for the high five. I replicated her gesture, and then we both laughed. Looking at her that moment I realized something. It's a misconception that woman is a weaker sex. Rather she has always been much stronger than the men. I couldn't even imagine myself experiencing what she had gone through at a tender age, and she narrated her story as if it had been an adventurous ride.

"Shall we go now?" she said and rose from the stairs.

As she started to climb up the stairs, I grasped her hand. She instantly pivoted in surprise. "Have you ever told this story to someone before?" I asked. I had to know this.

"After *Nana*, you are the second person I have told everything. I don't like it when people get sympathetic. I don't need their pity. I only want them to accept me as I am," she said.

"Why me then?" I asked. I could understand why she told everything to *Nana*, but why me? I couldn't fathom.

"Because you needed it," she shrugged, and I looked at her confused. Of course, I needed it, and it did affect me, but she couldn't know that. She would have met hundreds of disheartened people before, yet she didn't let anyone in. Then why me? She might have read the confusion on my face as she added, "We all are tied with invisible threads, and the other ends of those threads are tied to someone we are destined to cross path with. They may be known or unknown. When I saw you for the first time, I felt like you were holding the other end of one of many threads tied to me. I felt the tug the very first day I saw you. Like it wasn't just the casual encounter. Like we would be playing some role in each other's life. So I am just making sure it's for something better," she smiled slyly and I couldn't help mine too.

"Who told you all this?"

"*Nana*. He felt this way when he met me for the first time,"

"And what did you experience when you felt that way?" I asked out of curiosity. She scrunched her nose that I had started to find cute and then shook her head.

"I... I just felt something... in my stomach, and my... body and then in my... humph... I can't explain it," she waved her hand as she struggled to find the right words to describe the feeling. "It's a kind of déjà vu, like I already know and have met you before. I can't put it in words," she rambled and chewed her lower lip. Her face was flushed as if she had confessed something she wasn't supposed to. Then she laughed, embarrassed, and closed her eyes shut. I shook my head and laughed. It was a treat to watch that chatterbox short of words.

"Are you making fun of me, Adyant Lohani?" she narrowed her eyes at me playfully.

"Call me, Ady," I said.

"OMG! I can't believe I got the privilege so soon," she twirled clapping her hands teasingly, and this time I laughed aloud.

"Hey... but do keep your head straight. I am still not interested in you," she said, pointing the finger at me.

"I will keep that in mind," I said.

"I think it's time to start," she said glancing at her wristwatch and started climbing the stairs. I didn't know in which context she said that but for me, yes. It was time for the new beginnings as God had given the pen in my hand to write my own story.

CHAPTER 7

Down The Memory Lane

I honked the car incessantly as we were stuck in traffic, but no luck. The car couldn't even move an inch. After taking Riya's dress from the shop, we headed back to Manesar. It had already been an hour since we started, yet we couldn't even make our way across Delhi. I was getting frustrated amidst summer afternoon, traffic and repeated calls from Ekta. I hit the horn a few more time.

"Can you tell me how this repeated honking is going to help to get us through the traffic?" she asked, tilting her head in my direction.

"At least it's calming the exasperation," I answered.

"There are other ways too that are less noisy and more effective,"

"Yes. Gurudev. Teach me that too," I said mockingly and heard her giggling. I smiled at the sound. Did she know her laugh was better than any other technique to calm the anxiety?

"Take deep breathes. In and out. In and out," she said, mimicking the breathing in and out. "You will feel better," she added. I shook my head and honked for one more time.

"As if I don't know it already," I murmured. She laughed and then looked outside the window. Another few minutes passed, and we were yet stuck in the traffic. I glanced at her as she rolled down her window. I was about to tell her to close it as hot air wafted inside the car, but she beat me in that.

"You think that music and selling vegetables are related in anyway?" she asked, and I looked at the direction she was pointing to.

"No,"

"Look at him. He is playing the flute while at the same time selling vegetables," she gestured towards a vegetable seller who was playing trill on the instrument with utter perfection.

"I am trying to show you that nothing is irrelevant if you actually love doing it. So if you think that running a business and keeping your passion for music is like sailing in two boats, you may surely draw some inspiration from him," she said gesturing at the view outside.

I looked at the other vegetable seller standing beside him who was busy with the customer while the one playing the instrument had no customer.

"Yeah, right. And he is so engrossed in playing that he forgot to charm the customers," I said gesturing towards the customer who preferred to buy from the other vendor.

"Right," she said, scrunching her nose. "But still he looks so happy while the one with customers has a scowl on his face," she added. I looked again at them and tried to comprehend her inference. And then I looked at Riya who had this mischievous glint in her eyes. Unbuckling her seat belt, she clambered off the car. "Where are you going?" I asked astonished. "Well! You are wrong. He has caught my attention," she said and sprinted towards that vegetable seller. I liked that she never gave up on anything, be it life or a stupid argument. I watched it from the distance as she bought a few vegetables from him. After paying him, she took out a card and gave it to him. She said something that I couldn't hear because of the distance, which made that boy smiling ear to ear.

"What did you give him?" I asked as she slid in the car again. She twirled in her seat to keep the vegetable bag on the back seat. "I gave him your visiting card," she said as she fastened her seat belt again. "Why?" I asked. "I told him to keep practicing and approach you after one year, so that you may hire him," she said, and my brows rose in amazement. "Do hire him. He is really good," she said and I couldn't hold my smile. I followed her gaze as she again glanced at the vegetable seller, who had another customer. Riya clapped her hands, "Look. Now he is getting attention too."

And I was no longer surer if she was convincing me, or a part of hers. I was so wrong about her. Not only me, but everyone was so wrong about her. Why do we get so judgmental without getting in another person's shoe? And there she was who didn't judge me even once. All she did was to show me the light when I assumed darkness was my life. Her ways of dealing with life may not be perfect, but at least she tried without giving up, without cursing the fate, and without accusing people who did bad to her. Her birth parents, did she ever think about them? She told me that she tried to search for them. Did she long for them? Or did she curse them for leaving her alone in this cruel world? Before I could stop, I found myself asking, "How do you feel about your birth parents?" And I saw the smile on her face vanishing slowly. "Ignore. You don't have to answer that." I said to make her comfortable.

"That's fine. Umm... How can you feel anything for someone when you don't even know them? When you have no idea about the circumstances they were in? Maybe they were helpless. Maybe they wanted a boy and keeping me would have ruined my mother's life. Maybe someone stole me, and they were told I died. Maybe I was an illegitimate child, and no one wanted me. There are a lot of scenarios, and unless I know why, I can't hate or love them. And yeah,

I watch a lot of Bollywood movies. Which genre you like in movies by the way?" With that, she tactfully changed the conversation, and it kept on going until we reached the destination. She jumped off the car as soon as I parked it. I watched her running towards the front porch where a *Dholi* was playing the *dhol* and people were dancing on the beats. She effortlessly joined the group and danced in cadence. I clambered off and walked towards the congregation. I stood among the audience and watched her dancing. It was a treat to watch her swaying on the beats without the care of the world. A surge of pang hit my gut at the thought that no one except me could see the pain and loneliness behind that megawatt smile. One of the boys held her hand and pretended to dance as a couple. She laughed as he twirled her. People here would again be judging her for her actions just like I was doing this morning, but I knew now that she was as pure as the driven snow. She looked at me and beckoned to join the dance with a quick motion of her hand. I waved my hand in no. I was more than okay being her audience. She then winked at me facetiously and started throwing flying kisses my way. If I hadn't known her the way I knew her now, it could have made me cringe, but I laughed aloud at her this gesture throwing my head back. She too laughed. We kept laughing, looking at each other.

"I can't believe this," I came out of our little laughing contest as I heard someone murmuring beside me. I looked in the direction and found Ekta glowering at Riya.

"Congratulations! I guess now you too are one in the line of her conquests," she said looking at me this time.

"You are presuming, Ekta, when you know nothing about her," I said, returning her glare.

"Of course, you are a boy. I am a girl. I will never know her the way you know her," she said, shaking her head in disgust and then disappeared inside the house. When did it become so difficult to talk to her? She was the one to understand me so well. Perhaps she wasn't wrong either.

Maybe Riya was just the same with me as she was with any other boy here. Maybe I was one of those boys who fell for her charm. But it felt different. It didn't matter if this was the last time I was seeing her; I knew in my heart of hearts that she would always be there in my mind. She had captured a piece of my heart that would forever belong to her.

I looked back at Riya and found her laughing with someone else this time. Was it because she was flirtatious? Or was it her way to get the attention that she had never gotten by just being nice? *People are selfish. Love is selfish.* Her words echoed in my head. Did she really mean them? Or it was just her way to express the longing for people and love. We often assume that we don't seek approval from other people, but deep down, we have this urge to be accepted and loved by people. It's a basic emotional need. Someone blessed with the loved one around, doesn't realize what he or she has until it's gone. And the one who has no one, try to draw attention. For someone seeking the affability desperately, the line between admiration and ignominy gets blur. They try to get attention anyhow, from anywhere they can get it. And we, rather than understanding their need, judge them.

I looked at my watch. It was half-past four in the evening. Exactly eight hours since I got to know her, and a lot had changed in those hours. It was a new me who could see things differently now. All of a sudden everything felt plausible. My situation was yet the same; nonetheless, it felt like the things that were troubling me some time ago had suddenly alleviated. My mind started playing with the words, and I had an urge to note them down. It could be the lyrics of a song that I was undoubtedly going to dedicate to her. Leaving her alone there in her world, I sprinted towards my room and jotted down lyrics humming them aloud. She wasn't the perfect girl, but it was her imperfections that had enticed me the most. As I finished the lyrics, one more thing I realized. I didn't just like her; I had fallen in love with her.

CHAPTER 8

Down The Memory Lane

I rolled my shoulders to adjust the grey suit jacket as I ran down the stairs to attend the wedding reception. My whole attention was on the phone call that I had received a few minutes ago. My mother wasn't well, and I had to leave for Dehradun in a few hours. But before that, I needed to fix a few things. First on the agenda was to meet my friends and tell them the news that I was ready to give our band a shot. I wanted to experience their response face to face. Second, I wanted to tell Riya that whatever we had developed in this short time wasn't going to end here. Now, as I had found her, I wasn't ready to let her go just like that. I needed her contact details so that I could at least remain in touch with her.

The arrangements for the wedding were made in the open garden outside. The music from the live orchestra blared in my ears as I came out. The bride and groom were already on the stage. I headed to them to extend my best wishes. I did see my friends on the way, but they ignored me, and my heart didn't ache this time at their gesture because I knew it was going to end soon. I had an urge to stop and talk to them, but it had to wait for some more time. I wished the couple and was posing for a photograph when I saw Riya in the crowd. One look at her and I forgot where I was standing. I couldn't take my eyes off of her. She looked beautiful in that saree, just as I had imagined her. With her hair open in loose curls, she looked impeccable. She too caught my eye and waved at me. As I padded towards her, she met me halfway.

"How am I looking?" she asked, twirling on her heel to show me her dress.

"I have no words," I said in appreciation.

"I know! I look good! I am getting compliments, you know. I also saw people sighing in relief… and also a few in disappointment," she giggled.

"Such a hypocrite people. Whatever I wore was indecent before, and now, despite all this skin show I am decently dressed," she said derisively, gesticulating the gap between her blouse and saree skirt.

"Earlier I was as bad as a devil now they look at me as if I am a deity. I don't understand how you could judge someone just by his/her clothes. Clothes can't be the testimony of someone's character. Can they?" she asked without actually being in the conversation as she started walking beside me. Her eyes wandered here and there looking for something God knew what.

"Come here," I held her elbow and cornered her to the side where a server was serving the sweets.

"Can you tell me something about this?" I gestured towards a sweet kept in the platter.

"What nonsense! It's a Barfi," she replied.

"Tell me something about it," I asked.

"Don't tell me you never had one. Well! It's milk-based sweet with dry fruits and all, and it tastes sweet," she said.

"How can you judge it without tasting it? It's not a good thing to make an opinion about something just by its appearance. Isn't it?" I asked, raising my brow.

"Haha…You are saying anything to prove me wrong," she said, laughing.

"I am not proving you wrong, Riya. I am just trying to tell you why it is so," I said, slipping my hands inside my pant pockets.

"Well! In that case, I could tell about it because I have tasted it before," she responded, giving me her full attention now.

"Maybe. But you haven't tasted this one, and you are making an opinion based on your previous experiences. That's what my point is. I am not saying the way you dress up is a bad thing, but we are raised to believe that traditional is respectable, even if it shows more skin than that of western. Things have already changed a lot, and maybe a few decades' later things would further change. No one will be bothered, even if someone walks unclothed. But as of now, it is what it is. And there is nothing bad in respecting other's opinion too," she opened her mouth to say something, but I stopped her by holding my hand up, "and trust me, I admire you for making an effort to respect other's views." She again opened her mouth but didn't say anything, and then she nodded, spreading her warm smile.

"Oh shit! I forgot something. Gotta go," she said and started to sprint all of a sudden.

"Hey, what happened? Where are you going?" I yelled after her.

"See you later, Adyant," she said, waving her hand and dismissing me without looking back. I sighed and shook my head. I didn't even get the chance to tell her what I wanted to say. I started for my next mission— breaking the news to my bandmates. I had just taken a few steps when I heard an announcement from the podium where the orchestra was playing earlier. It caught my attention because of the voice that blared from the speakers.

"Ladies and Gentlemen, I am sorry to interrupt you all. We have an upcoming rock star here. And I wouldn't want to miss the opportunity to have him sing a song for all of us. Please, welcome Adyant Lohani who is going to regale us all with his magical voice," Riya's voice echoed catching everyone's attention. And all of a sudden, I froze there with cold feet. I hadn't expected that neither I was prepared. But as the people started clapping and I saw her smiling on the stage waiting for me, I felt confident. This was the time. I padded up to the podium and saw her smile turning into mischievous one. She handed over the mike to me as I stood beside her on the stage.

"I just want to make sure you won't renege upon your promise. Drastic times call for drastic measures. Get ready, Adyant. It's time to pull out all the stops," she whispered in my ear before leaving the stage and joining the audience.

"Thank you so much, Riya, for this opportunity. She just exaggerated calling me a Rock star, but now I assure the day is not far. When? How? I have no idea, but I have my friends… my team. Shaun, Nik and Manik, I am sorry for being a disappointment to all of you, but I am in. And I can't do it without you guys. We want it bad, and we will make it happen," I said, keeping my hand on my heart. I tried to search them in the audience but couldn't find any of them. I took the guitar from one of the artists and cleared my throat before strumming a few warm-up chords. Then I started the opening melody of the song that I had created a few hours ago. I started singing the song looking into her eyes. I wanted to tell her that this song was for her.

Broken and alone

When the hope was gone

I was looking for a ray

Somewhere lost in the way

Then I saw you

And I saw the light

So lustrous

so bright

where you have been all this time

If you were here, luck would have been all mine...

ooo... ooo... all mine, all mine... luck would have been all mine...

As my voice echoed in the air, I closed my eyes, living and breathing the lyrics. I poured my soul into the song reaching the high and low notes with my fingers picking the chords. I felt a rustle behind me, and when I looked back, I found Shaun easing down behind the drum set and twirling the sticks between his fingers before he began the magic with an upbeat tempo. Then my attention turned from him to Nik as he took the bass guitar from the artist. He put the strap over his head and adjusted it on his body before jogging beside me on the stage, maniacally grinning with his dimples popping out. Something he often did when he was happy. He then joined in rhythm with the Shaun and me. Manik too strode to stand beside Nik holding the other mike and providing the vocal harmony as I warbled the lyrics *all mine... all mine*. It wasn't the first time we were performing together on the stage, but this time it felt surreal, just like a new beginning. I looked at Riya and found her bouncing in ecstasy. I continued the song as my friends played the instruments in cadence with the lyrics.

I assumed I wouldn't survive

what I was going through

all I needed was

those eight hours with you

you saw all that in my eyes,

no one has ever seen.

You touched me there,

no one could ever be

where you have been all this time

If you were here, luck would have been all mine...

ooo... ooo... all mine, all mine... luck would have been all mine...

I let my friends add their magic to the song with their talent in music styling. Manik took over the mike as he did a quick rap, making the song more striking. Our enthusiasm rose further as we saw the audience swaying their hands in appreciation. The upbeat of our effort was evident on the faces of the audience. As if my eyes were trained, it found those pair of eyes, who had stolen a piece of my heart. She was no longer wearing the smile she initially had on her face. Instead, I saw the anguish on that beautiful face that I couldn't comprehend why. My heart thumped, thinking that perhaps she didn't like my open display of affection, but I continued because it was now or never kind of situation for me. I kept my eyes locked with her as I played the lead on my guitar. And with that eye-lock, something shifted between us. Something so intense and profound. It wasn't just the feeling of tied invisible thread, but a strong pull too as if all my nerves were attuned to her. I couldn't blink dreading that it would ruin the moment. It would break the important conversation we were having through our eyes. I let that energy pass between us as I sang the next stanza.

Everything was true whatever you said

that we were tied with an invisible thread

In your eyes, I see the sky of my dreams,

A smile on your lips makes my heart beam

now as I have found you

I won't let you go

What your presence meant to me,

Now that I know

where you have been all this time

If you were here, luck would have been all mine...

ooo... ooo... all mine, all mine... luck would have been all mine...

I closed my eyes as my fingers strummed the last notes frantically. I felt the vibrations in my chest as Shaun drummed in rhythm. We were greeted with the thunderous applaud as we ended the song. I opened my eyes to look where I had seen Riya last, but she wasn't there. I tried to search in the audience but couldn't find her anywhere. Shaun, Nik and Manik came towards me and hugged me tightly.

"Thanks, Bro," Shaun said, patting my back.

"Don't thank me, just forgive me for behaving like an asshole,"

"Already done. Now we need to sit down and make a strategy," he replied as we started off the stage.

"I know, but now I need to head back home. My mother is not well," I said and saw the worry clouding their faces.

"Hey, nothing to worry. It just that she is still in trauma after Dad's demise," I added.

"You want us to come with you?" Manik asked.

"No buddy, I will handle it. You guys make a plan, and I will arrange the funds we need for our first launch. Being in my Dad's business for some time, I have made a few links. They will be happy to sponsor us," I said.

"That's great, but earlier you refused to use your dad's link for any sponsorship," Nik asked.

"Yeah... but someone told me there is nothing bad in using people and creating the opportunity," saying it aloud, I realized how she had influenced my life with her beliefs. Dragging myself out from her thoughts, I added, "And moreover, they will invest only if they see the benefit. So there's nothing bad," They all nodded, and we again huddled each other in hugs.

"Now I need to find someone before I leave," I said, readying myself to find Riya.

"It's that girl. Isn't she?" Nik grinned at me, displaying those dimples. I didn't reply and sprinted to find her. I searched for the whole venue but couldn't find her. My heart ached with the knowledge that I might have hurt her. I asked Esha, but she too had no idea. Disheartened, I came back to my room to collect my luggage. I decided to check her in her room before leaving, but she wasn't there either. I had just exited the house and was on my way to the parking when I heard her.

"Again sneaking out, Adyant Lohani? Without saying bye?" she asked. I swivelled to look at her and found her smoking a cigarette. I drew closer to her and took the cigarette from her to put it out. She looked at my foot as it crushed the cigarette butt.

"Trust me. I did look for you," I replied, looking up and smiling at her.

"Hmm..." she said and pursed her lips. It was evident from her expressions that she wanted to say something but was in a quandary.

"I figured it out that you didn't like our performance," I said, trying to start the conversation.

"That's not true. It was stupendous. What made you think so?" she asked.

"You left before we ended," I retorted.

"Umm... I got a call and... it was so loud there. I had to leave to attend it," she said. The way her eyes wandered here and there, I knew she was lying.

"Must be an important one then," I jibed.

"Yeah... It was from my boyfriend," she said, looking down. She never looked into the eyes when lying. Something I had learnt about her. My inner voice screamed to retort, but what was the point. Her lie indicated that she didn't want me, and I wasn't the one to impose myself on her. I nodded in response.

"I was wondering if I could get your contact number or email address so that we might remain in touch," I asked hesitantly.

"I can't share either of them," she said with her eyes down. Her cheek grew red. But then suddenly she looked up at me and added, "But I do remember your number, and I will call you the day you will make your name in the singing." As she said that I saw the glint in her eyes returning. I smiled, though it stung that she didn't want to be in touch with me. I mirrored her previous gesture as I raised my crooked finger towards her, "Pinky promise?"

She smiled and entwined her finger with mine. Who had known then it would take her six years to keep the promise, and that too for an entirely different reason! I held her finger in mine as I voiced my fear, "What if I fail?"

I didn't know why I asked her this. Maybe I needed her validation. Or maybe I was looking for her comforting words. I expected her to deliver a failure-success speech, but what she said made me adore her even more. I felt determined.

"You won't," just the two words, but the way she said those words was emboldening. She stated them as if she could see the future, and she was sure of it. Sometimes all it takes is someone to trust our capabilities more than us. She had confidence in me more than I had on myself. I could fail myself, but I would never let fail her.

"Ok then, bye," I said as I took a step back.

"Adyant," she whispered. I found confusion etched on her face. Then it dawned on me she was here to say something that she hadn't mentioned yet.

"What is it, Riya?" I asked, looking back and forth in her eyes. She straightened her back and cleared her throat.

"I don't want to be rude, but I would rather prefer someone with a gun in hand than a guitar," she said, and I felt the first crack in my heart. She kept looking at me for a response, but when she didn't get any, she swallowed. She took a hesitant step towards me. Was it really what she wanted to say? Why did she look so unsure then? "You are a good boy, Adyant. It's just I am more into the bad ones. Trust me. It's my bad," she added, picking the nonexistent lint from my shoulder.

"So you are rejecting me?" I said, and her eyes darted on mine. I smiled impishly before adding, "By the way, what made you think that I was proposing to you?" I acted clueless veiling the hurt under a playful smile, and saw her cheeks turning further red. The blush was an expression I had never witnessed on her face before. She looked cute.

"I just... you sang... I thought..." She trailed off.

"It's fine, Riya. I will keep it in mind," I said, smiling.

"All the best," she said, holding her thumb up. I nodded and pivoted towards my car. I felt the blazing pain in my gut as I took the steps away from her. I opened the deck lid to keep the luggage. As I closed it, I looked at her to take in her last glimpse. *Her last*. Even though she told me she would call me, I knew somewhere in my heart, she wouldn't. I wanted to memorize her features so that I could recreate her in my mind later. She was beautiful in her own way. Her features weren't sharp, yet she had that charismatic aura around her that exuded the exquisiteness. Her eyes big and brown, same as the color of her hair, her nose small but pointed, her chin had a dimple. Her complexion wasn't fair, but her skin was smooth. Her lips weren't plump, but they curved beautifully when she smiled. I padded towards her. There was still something she hadn't told me.

"What happened?" she asked, confused, as I stood in front of her.

"What's your dream, Riya?" I asked the question that was troubling me. I had asked her earlier too, but she said it was something that wasn't in her hands. Her response had made me more curious, but I couldn't ask her then. She smiled, and I noticed it didn't reach her eyes.

"To have a family," she whispered, and I instantly felt her pain. She might have seen that on my face as she started laughing nervously.

"I know it's stupid. I dream of something that other people take for granted. But it is what it is," she shrugged, looking away from me.

We never realize the importance of what we have until we see someone yearning for the same. Our reality might be someone's unfulfilled dream.

"Bye, Riya. Take care. And always remember, I am yet to play my role in your life. Do reach me out whenever you are in need. Okay?" I asked, and she nodded in response. Without glancing back, I left her there, promising myself that I wouldn't give up on my dream till my last breathe, if not for myself then for her.

"You have got a real dream and talent too."

Her words reverberated in my head as I drove the car, and now I realized the inference. She pushed me because she didn't have a real dream in life. Her dream was a necessity that she wasn't blessed with.

Present Day

Grand Finale, *The Singing Star*

Mumbai

"Wasn't it the best dance performance you have ever seen? A big round of applause for the contestant of our dance reality show," the hostess says after the performance of contestants from some other show. They play a prank with one of the contestants, and the audience burst into a laugh. Memories have clogged my mind so much that I fail to comprehend any of it.

"Now it's the most exciting time of the event when the judges will perform on the stage. I invite our judges here for the last performance of the show, and then we are going to announce the results," the crowd clapped and cheered. My mind again went back to the day that opened another chapter of my life—the day when I met her for the second time.

CHAPTER 9

Down The Memory Lane

New Delhi

January 2011

I waited outside the complex in my car where Riya had told me to meet. I was a bit early here, just in case. When my watch displayed four-thirty, I parked the car and clambered off. Not wanting to attract any attention, I pulled the peak of my ball cap on my head to cover my face a bit. I looked here and there for her, but there wasn't any sign of Riya. It was five minutes later when I heard someone calling me from behind, and I instantly recognized the voice.

Riya.

When I pivoted to get her glimpse, I was taken aback. She had wrapped her entire head and face in a scarf. Only her eyes were visible.

"Hey," I said.

"Can we sit somewhere?" she said, her voice muffled as her mouth was covered in a scarf. I looked around, trying to find another restaurant where we could sit. I assumed she wouldn't want to talk at her workplace.

"Shall we go there?" I gestured towards the restaurant. She hesitated for a moment but then nodded, seeing that I was studying her response. She was acting oddly, and it had started bothering me. We sat across each other in the restaurant. She kept fumbling with the corner of menu card looking down. She was nervous. I took the initiative to start the conversation.

"Why are you dressed like a dacoit? Or are you on a secret mission?" I asked jokingly. It worked as her eyes smiled and she unveiled the lower part of her face pulling the scarf down.

"Did I scare you? It's just Delhi weather doesn't suit me. I get tan so easily," she tried to justify.

"It's evening," my reply was quick. What was wrong with her?

"Oh! Actually, I was out the whole day and didn't get time to take it off. It's quite cold anyway. So I just kept it wrapped," she rambled.

'*I love to get tan. You know tanned bodies are a sign that someone has actually lived his or her life,*' I remembered her words. She didn't care about tan in peak summers, and now she was behaving as if she was allergic to the sun.

"It's okay. You don't have to justify yourself," I said, and she sighed. She was hiding something... or maybe she was hiding from someone. I didn't try to prod further. I didn't want to sound inquisitive.

"So? How's everything going?" I changed the topic.

"Good. All is good," she joggled her head.

"Umm... Adyant, I need a job. Can you help me to find one?" she said and waited for my response before adding anything further.

"Of course, I can help you. Rather the recruitments are just going to start at my company. If you are interested, I can see where I can fit you," I lied. Recruitments had already been over a month ago.

"There is a problem," she said hesitantly, as she again started fumbling with the menu.

"What's wrong?" I held my breath as I waited for the response.

"I don't have my documents with me. You know, not a single one. Is that going to be a problem?"

"No. It won't be a problem, but can I ask where they are?" I asked clearly remembering that she was pursuing her graduation when I had met her last.

"I... I lost them. Umm... I was coming here by... train when someone stole my bag on the way. I don't have anything now," I nodded my head, seeing a lie all over her face. The way her voice wavered and eyes danced here and there. I knew this story was made up.

What was she hiding? I had to know, but she wasn't willing to share, and I didn't want to push her. But I could interview her; she had asked me for the job. I started asking the questions to get something out from her.

"Do you have any work experience?" I asked, hoping this single question will answer many of my doubts.

"Yes. I have experience in web designing,"

"That's great. Which company?"

"Umm... I worked as a freelancer,"

"Okay. Where?"

"Lucknow,"

"Ok. I think you may help us in improving our website as we have just started the online sale for *TingTong* toys,"

"Yes. I can do that. Trust me. I am good at that," I saw her eyes shining at my proposal.

"I don't doubt that," I said and was thinking what I could ask her next when she glanced at her watch and bolted up.

"I think I should leave. It's my shift time," she said.

"Riya, Can you come to my office tomorrow? Some formalities need to be done there only," I asked just making an excuse to meet her again. She hesitated for a moment tugging the strap of her bag on her shoulder.

"Your office? The same one? At what time?"

"Anytime you feel comfortable," I replied and noticed her doing some calculations mentally.

"Um… morning at eleven?"

"Perfect. See you then,"

"Sure," she smiled and turned to leave. She again pulled up the veil over her nose.

I kept staring at her back. She opened the exit door and then looked back. The look in her eyes told that she had something to say. I stood up and walked up to her.

"Is there something you want to say?" I asked.

"Umm… if I am going to work on your website, can I work from home?"

"We will discuss it tomorrow," I replied, and she left nodding at me once.

That whole evening, I fought the urge to go to the restaurant where she was working. She left me with more questions than answers. I still didn't have her contact information. And there was nothing I could do about it, except waiting for the next day. I came back to my apartment, still thinking about her. I didn't know if I was fascinated by the mystery she had created or was irritated. Why couldn't she tell me if something was bothering her?

I kept the takeout box of Biryani that I got packed from the same restaurant, on the kitchen slab, and called my mother. It had been a routine now, calling her every evening. After talking to Maa, I called Shaun. They had reached Maldives. I spoke to them as I switched on the geyser for a quick shower and took out clothes to change. After the dinner, I emailed my HR manager to keep ready an employee form by tomorrow, and also to accommodate a work from home employee. After watching Television for some time, I lazed on my bed as the exhaustion took over me and I fell in deep slumber.

The next day I sat on my leather chair in front of my mahogany wooden table. The employee form was already on my desk. I had a lot of other papers on the table those were demanding my attention. But I decided to take care of them after meeting Riya. Concentrating on anything else was hard. What was I? A teenager? I felt like the one where in reality, I was close to thirty. That's when something dawned on me, and I quickly dialled my secretary's number.

"Sir, how can I help you?" she asked as she picked the phone.

"Can you order a pizza with olives and baby corn?"

"Certainly, sir. Would you like to add some soft drinks or coffee or tea?"

"Coffee would be perfect. Make it for two." I said and ended the call.

My intercom buzzed again. It was from the secretary to inform me about Riya's arrival. My heart started pounding as the door opened.

"Hey," I said as I saw her entering my office. I rose from my seat and ambled to share a quick side hug. She wore cotton blue Kurti with her hair braided to one side and with no scarf today. She looked almost the same as she looked six years back except slight darkness around her eyes and her hair had grown longer.

"Please, have a seat," I forcibly moved my eyes away from her and pulled back a chair for her.

"I am sorry, but I am in a hurry! Can we make it quick?" she said as she made herself comfortable on the seat.

"Seems like you are always in a hurry," I mocked, and she smiled.

"What's wrong, Riya? Why do I feel you are hiding something from me?" I couldn't hold back my inquisitiveness.

"Nothing. Going through a bad phase. That's it," she laughed humorlessly shaking her head slightly.

"How can I help to make it better?" I asked.

"You are already helping," she said. I nodded my head, barring myself from further meddling. I slid the employee form towards her and asked her to fill the details. Next few minutes, she kept her head down, filling the details in the form. And I took my time to study her profile. Time hadn't touched her at all because she still looked the same, but I couldn't deny that her demeanor had changed drastically. Her brows furrowed at something she read in the form and she shifted in her seat. After pausing for a moment she started scribbling again, and I wondered what could it be that made her so uncomfortable?

"What am I suppose to fill in these columns? I don't have an address for now as I am crashing in a hotel. Neither a contact number as I lost my phone too." she said.

"Do you want us to provide company accommodation?" I asked. We hadn't done that before, but I could do this for her.

"You do that? That would be really nice," she said astonished.

"And here," I said and opened my drawer to take out a mobile phone and a laptop I had arranged for her.

"This is your official phone and laptop," I slid both of them towards her. She hesitated before touching them.

"Is it something you do for every employee?" she asked.

"Yes. We provide the phone and laptop, especially the one working from home," I said, which was a half-truth.

"Does that mean I can work from home?" she said, straightening her back, and I could sense the elation in her gesture.

"Yes," I smiled.

Once she entered the last few details in the form, she handed it back to me. The office boy entered the room with two cups of coffee and a large pizza box. He placed it on the table and left. I kept the form that Riya had given me aside and looked towards her. "It's your favourite one with olives and baby corns. See, I can afford it now," I said jokingly, and she smiled.

"You remembered?" she asked.

"I remember everything about you, Riya. It's just you who forgot to keep your promise. Or maybe you just don't consider me successful yet," I said as I added sugar in my coffee.

"Nothing like that. I was so happy for you, Adyant. It's just I couldn't muster the courage to call you, dreading that I would mess up everything. I don't know why," she said with her gaze on the table and burrow furrowed. She seemed lost momentarily. Why did she say that? I couldn't understand. Was it because she didn't want our paths to cross again? Shaking the thought out of my head, I concentrated on the moment.

"Now leave it and let's enjoy the Pizza," I said as I opened the flap of the box. The delicious smell wafted, and I heard her moaning.

"Seems mouthwatering. But I really have to go," she said as she got up holding the strap of her bag on her shoulder.

"Riya, sit down and have it. I specially ordered it for you," I implored.

"Then can you get it packed? I will take it with me. But I really can't afford any more time," she said obstinately.

"Okay," I capitulated and hit the call bell to call the office boy and get it packed.

Riya didn't sit back and looked around my office. Her gaze fell on my guitar, propped up against the wall, and she smiled.

"Remember?" she said, darting her eyes at me, and I nodded in response, smiling.

"Can't believe it's been six years. It seems like it happened yesterday," she added.

"True," I said and saw her eyes clapped on the boxes of dolls lined up in the corner of my room.

"That's our new product. A talking doll," I explained and moved to demonstrate her one of our best products. The product had just arrived after testing and was yet to hit the market. I opened one box and took out a raven-haired, blue-eyed doll. I started demonstrating it as I saw Riya excited seeing it. It also reminded me that she had been fascinated with the dolls as a child. I switched it on, and she immediately started speaking in a mechanical voice, "Hello, I am Veeny. What's your name?"

"Hello Veeny, I am Ady," I replied to the doll.

"It's nice to meet you, Ady. How can I help you? Do you want me to play rhymes for you or sing a song," she asked and I switched it off.

"A few poems and songs are already stored in this one. We can also feed several question and responses in it. Mother can even record the instructions, songs, poem or anything in her own voice, which is very comforting for kids, when the mother is not around," I demonstrated proudly.

"That's so nice," she took the doll from me and looked at it with curiosity.

"I wish I could..." she trailed off, suddenly looking despondent, but she quickly recovered her smile as she added, "How much it cost?" she asked.

"You can have one. These are just the sample pieces for testing purpose. Use it and let me know me how it works?" I lied.

"Are you sure?"

"Pretty much. And as you have plenty of things with you now, my driver will drop you to your hotel. I will call to inform you when you can start working," I said.

"Okay," she said, nibbling her lower lip.

"Are you working in that restaurant today too?"

"Yes, I have to inform them a week before resigning. I will do it today,"

"Great,"

"I should leave now. See you soon," she said.

"Definitely," I said and then she was gone.

I had a look at her credential that didn't give me much information except her qualification that she had mentioned as Engineering in Information Technology and the name of her institute, her age- Twenty-five years, Marital status- single and many other random things that weren't of my any interest. I kept it aside and started working on the next assignment that was waiting for my attention.

CHAPTER 10

Down The Memory Lane

Such a stupid, desperate bastard, I am! I cursed myself as I found me standing outside the restaurant in the evening where Riya worked. *Just turn and get the fuck out of here before she sees you.* A voice in my head argued, and I knew it was the right thing to do. We had been in the same situation before when I had scared her by showing my feelings openly. Seeing me here, she might get spooked and would try to push me away again. But I was too adamant about addressing that thought. I opened the door and entered. Craning my neck here and there, I tried to find her but didn't see her.

You still have time moron. She hasn't seen you yet. Get your ass back to your apartment. I heard my mind again. Snubbing all the voices, I found an empty table for myself and waited for some attendant. A saccharine voice greeted me a moment later, "What can I get you, sir," she asked. It wasn't Riya, and a part of me was happy that it wasn't her. Coming across her as a stalker or someone too desperate was the last thing I wanted.

"A cappuccino with grilled sandwiches," I ordered looking at the menu. Though my purpose of visiting this place was completely different, I wanted to look genuine in case Riya saw me. The waitress nodded and strolled back.

I looked around and found many families enjoying their food. It was a typical family kind of restaurant where people came just to have a good time. I noticed there was neither an open terrace arrangement nor karaoke that day. Maybe it was just for the New Year eve. The door opened again, and I saw three rowdies entering the restaurant. They looked odd considering the kind of crowd this place had. They particularly caught my attention because of their chafed looks and discourteous attitude, as they strode here and there looking for something. They stopped a waiter and asked him something to which he gestured towards the front desk. I shifted my gaze from them to the waitress as she placed my order on the table. I looked up at her as she was still standing there. She quietly kept a handkerchief and a pen beside the tray. Puzzled, I gazed at her again.

"Can I get the autograph? And don't worry, I won't tell anyone that you are here," she said smiling.

"Of course," I mumbled and signed the handkerchief for her.

"Thank you so much, sir. Anything else you want?" I could hear the elation in her voice.

"Nothing for now. Can you tell me where's the washroom?" I asked her, realizing the need to wash my hands.

"At the left of the front desk," she answered.

I got up and sauntered towards the washroom. As I reached near the front desk, I overheard one of the rowdies yelling at the male receptionist, "What do you mean you can't tell us?" I shifted my gaze to them and beheld receptionist's panicked face.

"I am sorry, sir. But I am not supposed to give any information regarding our employees. You may talk to the manager about this," he answered timidly. I didn't know what made me curious that I padded towards them, but halted in my track as my eyes examined the photograph in one rowdy's hand. I instantly broke out in cold sweat, seeing Riya's picture on it. I looked around and found her standing just behind them. Her face was white as if she had seen a ghost. She stood there frozen, I quickly covered her with my body as those rowdies turned right, towards the manager's room. I kept my hand at her back and guided her towards the passageway that led to the washroom. I dragged her inside the staff restroom and bolted it, finding no one inside.

"What's wrong, Riya?" I asked as I saw her trembling. She didn't say anything.

"Do you want me to take you away from them?" I asked, and she nodded instantly as a tear escaped her eye. She quickly wiped it with her hand.

"I need my bag," she said, readying her to get out of the washroom, but jerked back as someone knocked on the door. Petrified, she instantly held my arm. The bang on the door made us jump again.

"Open the door. It's me," A male voice wafted in, making Riya exhaling a sigh of relief. She moved and opened the door. It was the same front desk receptionist holding Riya's bag. "Take this, and get out of here as soon as possible. I have opened the emergency exit," he said, handing over the bag to Riya. The concern was etched on his face.

"Please, don't tell them about me," Riya requested in her shaky voice.

"Of course, but what are you up to? They seem dangerous," he said, and Riya looked down embarrassed.

"Don't worry. I will keep them distracted for a while. Be safe," I instantly saw green as he placed his hand on her shoulder. In reflex, my hand flew at her back.

"Who is he?" He asked, looking back and forth between Riya and me.

"He is a friend," she replied.

"We have to be quick, and shall get out of here before they talk to the manager and come back looking for you," I said, and she nodded. We exited the restaurant unscathed using the emergency exit that was just next to the washroom. Riya took out her scarf from the bag and wrapped it around her face. Soon we were inside my car as I drove as fast as I could to get her away. I did notice her right hand buried inside her bag all the time. Perhaps it was something that comforted her. When we were far enough, I asked her the question that was troubling me, "Who were they, Riya?"

She sighed and closed her eyes before answering, "My husband's people."

It came as a bolt from blue, turning me flabbergasted. My heart started beating erratically with hurt, anger, confusion and don't know what.

Her husband?

She was married? I had no right to think that way, yet it felt like I got cheated. I counted in my head to gain a scrap of composure, yet the hurt clung like a leech sucking all the rationality out of me. Before the absurdity could take over me, I buried the desire to say and ask anything further. I concentrated on manoeuvring the car.

"Oh my God!" she yelled all of a sudden. Her hand flew to her mouth instantly, and her eyes widened in horror. "If they know where I work, they might know where I live," she added.

"Maybe," I replied, glancing at her frequently to know what was bothering her.

"I need to go home," she said eyeing blankly at the dashboard. She looked frightened as if some dreadful scenario was running her mind.

"It's dangerous, Riya. We shouldn't go there. Right now, nothing is more important than your safety" I replied.

"Yeah, it's dangerous! I can't put your life in danger! I have to do it myself, stop the car!" She said as she fumbled clumsily with the car lock to open it. I had my car child-locked.

"Stop the car and open this damn door, Adyant. I need to go home," she howled. I stopped the car, parking it on the side of the road. Since the time I had known her, this was the first I had seen her so disheartened, so helpless. A part of me wanted to take her in arms and soothe her. She again tried to fight the door, when it didn't open she held her head in her arms and buried it in her knees propping them up.

"Let me go home, please," she cried.

"Give me direction, Riya. I am taking you there," I said as I revved the engine.

"No. You can't come with me! It's dangerous! I will take a taxi from here," she lifted her head and looked up at me obstinately with her teary eyes.

"If you want to go there, we are going together! Otherwise, I am not going to let you skate on the thin ice all alone," I said firmly. This time she didn't argue and gave me directions. The whole way, I could feel the hysteria and anxiety weaving around her as she trembled like a leaf. I didn't know what was there, but whatever it was, Riya considered it more important than her life. After half an hour, I parked the car outside an old building. She had lied to me that she stayed in a hotel. As we moved into society, I noticed there was no security outside. The walls looked like they could crumble at any moment. Several people were living there as I could see some of the flats with lights on, yet it was a poorly maintained society. I found it highly unsafe, considering the area. It wasn't a place worth living.

"You live here?" I asked, surprised.

"This was the only place I could afford," she answered as she rushed inside the building and started climbing up the stairs. I followed her. On the second floor, she hastily took out a key from her bag and fumbled clumsily with the lock. Considering the status of the door, it didn't even need a lock. One could easily break in just by one strong push. I took the keys from her hand. The way her hands were trembling, I doubted she would be able to open it. I unlocked the door, tugging on the handle before yanking it open. I entered first, and Riya was just behind me—She flicked on the light— and what I saw in front of me made me freeze on the spot. A curly head little girl was sleeping on the futon perched in one corner of the room. She had cuddled the talking doll I had given to Riya the same day. Riya rushed to her and took the little girl in her arms. I was too shocked to move. I closed my eyes in disbelief at another ridiculous lie that Riya had told me. The sudden surge of hurt laced with anger propelled me to move forward towards them. I kept looking at the two girls as they cuddled each other in a comforting hug.

"What happened, Mumma? Why are you crying?" the little girl asked as she held Riya's face in her small hands.

"Nothing baby girl. Mumma just missed you so much," Riya said trying to smile through her tear-filled eyes.

"I missed you too. You know, I ate the whole Pizza. It was so yummy. Can you bring a pizza tomorrow too?" the little girl asked in her mellifluous voice. Riya glanced at me once and then lowered her eyes as if she was ashamed. I felt my anger alleviate as the little girl looked up, and her eyes met mine. It was then when I noticed she was the replica of her mother. A full and genuine smile spread over my face as I step towards them and lower myself onto the haunches. The little girl shrieked as she hid her face in the crook of her mother's neck.

"He is a friend, Baby girl. He sent you this doll and Pizza," Riya appeased her by caressing her back.

"Hey, I am Ady," I said, and she turned her head to look at me. Even though I was a bit shocked, I couldn't help the smile that curved my lips as I saw those beautiful eyes crinkling in a smile.

"I am Nitya," she said.

Present Day

Grand Finale, The Singer Star

Mumbai

Loud thundering applause transports me back to the event. I look back at the stage and find all the twelve contestants there. I silently chastise myself for not paying attention to the most important event in my daughter's life. But I know that subconsciously I am registering every detail of the event and after some years I will be replaying this evening in my head with all the details, same as I am replaying now. She isn't my biological daughter, and it hurts me every time I think that it's not my blood running in her veins. But I made sure to substitute it with all of my love. She still has the same spark in her eyes that I had seen nine years back. My chest blazes with the pain, thinking how much this little soul has gone through in her small life. I had felt an instant connection with her then. A déjà vu moment in Riya's terms, as if she had the other end of the thread connected to me.

"It's a playtime now. We are going to play a musical game with our champs and have a little fun. Are you guys excited?" host announced and all the contestants cheered up.

Game.

The word gets stuck in my mind, and I wonder how life plays games with us? I didn't even know then that there are two girls born somewhere who are going to steal a part of my heart forever. Life has never been the same since she entered my life with her little feet, but I wouldn't want it any other way. My mind goes again back to that dirty room where I had found this bright and thriving little soul on the futon. There was so much in those beguiling eyes that I couldn't help falling in love with her instantly.

CHAPTER 11

Down The Memory Lane

"Thank you for the Doll and Pizza. I loved it so much!" Nitya said and cuddled the Doll in her arms.

"Tomorrow we are going to do more Pizzas and more dolls," I said, and those eyes lit up with excitement.

"Really?" she asked grinning ear to ear, and I nodded.

"Now baby girl, we are going to some other city. Mumma didn't like this city," Riya said to Nitya. I opened my mouth to ask something to Riya, but she shut me up with just one word, "Later."

"You get your things packed. We need to get out of this place fast," I said, and Riya sat Nitya on the futon and headed to the almirah in the corner of the room.

"Are you going to play this game with us too?" Nitya asked.

"Umm... which game?"

"*Find a Princess*. I am the Princess, and I have to hide because bad people are looking for me. Mumma is the soldier. She protects the Princess. What role are you playing?" she asked me.

"Well! Princess, I have no idea yet," I said, pursing my lips.

"It's ok. Do you know the rules?" she asked, tilting her head and looking at me. I shook my head. She rolled her lips as if she was disappointed with me.

"Let me tell you the rules first. You can't cry aloud! You can't shout, you have to stay in the house, and you need to be brave because sometime you will have to stay alone at home. If you break the rule you are out, and you won't get to live in a castle," she said counting all the rules on her fingers and waiting for my nod at each sentence to make sure that I understood. I smiled, realizing that I wasn't the only one being lied. "I think I was already in this game, but your Mumma didn't tell me the rules," I jibed at her and Riya looked at me instantly.

"We are ready to go," Riya said as she held all her belongings, which included her handbag, a laptop bag and a shopping bag stuffed with clothes.

I picked up Nitya in my lap, and she came happily. I felt tingling as she kept her curly head on my neck. We hastily left that building and walked towards the exit warily. We made it to my car unscathed. I opened the passenger door for Riya, and she slid in, taking Nitya from me. I revved the engine, and soon we were on the road. I was thinking to take both of them to my apartment, when Riya said, "Can you drop us to ISBT? I will take a bus from there," Riya said, and I glared in her direction. I smiled as I spot Nitya's cute face in deep slumber.

"To where?" I asked.

"I don't know, but I can't stay here anymore," she replied.

"You know I considered you one of the intelligent, brave and wise girls, but you are as Dumb as a jackass," I couldn't handle the sudden surge of the angst. How could she be so irresponsible?

"Excuse me?" she darted her gaze at me wide-eyed.

"What do you think you are? A warrior? A superwoman?" Seriously, what was she thinking? She opened her mouth to argue, but I shut her up, "Not a word, Riya. You think you can run from one city to another, jobless, without a penny and without a place to crash in and to top that you have a daughter to look after too."

"I have money," she retorted, but I ignored her.

"You are coming with me tonight. We are going to talk, and tomorrow we will decide the next plan of our action," I said, and surprisingly she didn't argue. Perhaps she was too tired for that.

Was I doing the right thing? Taking her along with me when I had no idea about her situation? But I knew I could never have abandoned her to the bus stand knowing well she was in danger. It wasn't long before the gentle sway of the car rolling on the smooth highway road lulled her into slumber. I took advantage, and Instead of heading towards my Apartment, I drove to Dehradun. I wanted to protect her and change of the city seemed fitter than just changing the place. I kept driving the car grinning ear to ear. Life is so unpredictable. Two days back, I was yearning to see her just once, and now I was taking her my home. I didn't know what the future holds for us, but I decided to rejoice this very moment.

We had just crossed Meerut, when Riya woke up. She looked here and there disoriented and then her eyes darted at me, "Where are we heading?" she looked outside the window and then again snapped her gaze at me, "Aren't we going to your home in Delhi?"

"No. We aren't." I replied.

"Then where are you taking us?" she asked. I knew she would freak out if I told her about Dehradun. So I preferred to keep quiet.

"You can't take us anywhere without our consent. That's kidnapping," she exclaimed. Nitya held up her head from Riya's lap and then looked at me and then turned her gaze towards Riya.

"Mumma, is he playing the kidnapper in the game?" she asked, and I couldn't hold my laugh.

"No. Princess, I am playing hero in the game," I said grinning impishly.

"And I am the heroine as I am playing princess,"

"Yes. And your mom is that corrupt soldier we need to teach a lesson. She lies a lot," I said, looking straight at the road.

"I didn't lie. I didn't tell the truth, and that's different,"

"We can have a detailed debate on this if you want," I argued.

"No, thanks," she said, turning her head away from me.

"Are you hungry baby girl? Do you want me to grab something for you to eat?" I asked Nitya as I stopped my car in a petrol pump to fill in the tank. She nodded in response, and I smiled as I clambered off the vehicle. After filling the fuel, I grabbed sandwiches from a nearby shop. I did talk to my mother about me arriving home with Riya. I didn't tell her much because I still knew nothing about Riya's situation. I again manoeuvred the car onto the highway. We made Nitya sit on the back seat as she feasted and played with her Doll. I chose this moment to talk to Riya. Helping her without the knowledge of her situation was like shooting in the dark.

"Is the situation bad?" I asked. She stopped chewing her sandwich momentarily and then asked feigning innocence, "What?"

"You know what! Your situation with your husband." I asked, throwing a sideways glance at her.

"We didn't get along well," she said, looking out of the window.

"Is that the reason he sent goons to find you, and you were scared like you have seen a ghost? Is that what you mean?" I jibed. Whom was she kidding? I wasn't born yesterday.

"Can we talk about it later? I don't want to discuss anything in front of her," she said, gesturing towards Nitya with her eyes. I nodded in response. It was so stupid of me to ask this in front of Nitya. It was after midnight when I stopped the car in front of my house. The white exterior of the bungalow gleamed even more in the full moonlight, making it look like a castle. Well! These weren't my words. Nitya shrieked looking at the house and called it a castle. I honked in front of my gate and gatekeeper opened the door instantly. My mother was already waiting for us in the verandah. I introduced Riya and Nitya to my mother as we entered the drawing-room.

"Sorry Aunty, for coming here unannounced. Adyant didn't tell us where he was taking us," Riya said hesitantly. Perhaps she thought that my mother would be annoyed at their unexpected arrival. She certainly didn't know her. My mother was the kind of person who would shelter the world if it were in her hand.

"Consider it your own home, Riya. You don't need my permission to come and stay here ever," she said caressing Nitya's head.

"How old are you, dear?" she asked Nitya who hid her face in the crook of her mother's neck. When she didn't answer, Riya answered on her behalf, "She is three and a half. Just a bit tired and cranky right now," she justified.

"I can understand, let me arrange dinner for you. You may freshen up here," she gestured towards the guest room. I placed all the Riya's belongings to the Guest room and let them have some alone time to settle in. I came back to my mother and hugged her. It had been almost three months since I had seen her.

"Thank you Maa, for making her feel at home," I said, holding her shoulders.

"She brought my son back home, how could I have not?" she said taunting.

"Now that's rude. I would have come in a day or two here," I said.

"What's wrong?" she whispered gesturing towards the guest room.

"I don't know exactly. Maybe an abusive husband she is running from. I have no idea. It's just my speculation," I said, and she nodded.

"Help her. We can also take help from Chauhan Ji if need be," she said, and I nodded. Vikram Chauhan was my father's friend and Senior Superintendent of Police, Dehradun. We were still talking when Nitya opened the door of the guest room. She had changed her clothes to nightsuit and her hair tied in a ponytail. I smiled at her, and she hid behind the curtain.

"You think I can't find you, Princess?" I said and feigned to search her. I deliberately searched her behind the wrong curtain and then sighed when I didn't find her there. She giggled at my pretence and this time I picked her up in my arms. My house lit up with her laughter as I nuzzled her stomach. I saw the upshot on my mothers face too as she too started laughing. She took Nitya in her arms and kissed her forehead. "You look like a princess," she said.

"And you look like a Granny of my storybook," Nitya said and then she started narrating the story to my mother from her book. My mother took her to the dining table, made her sit on her lap and started feeding her. I smiled, looking at both of them. How easily they both had mingled up with each other. My trance was broken when I heard a rustle behind and saw Riya standing in the doorway, looking wistfully at the same panorama.

"Her own Grandmother never touched her," she whispered, and I turned to look at her. Her eyes welled up, but she tactfully hid it behind a mirthless smile. "Why?" I asked.

"Because she is my daughter," she said and then shook her head. "Just ignore. It's another Saas-Bahu story, nothing special," she shrugged and ambled towards dining table.

CHAPTER 12

Down The Memory Lane

I stirred in my bed as I heard a rap on my door. I tried but couldn't open my eyes. First, the happenings of the previous day and then the gruelling journey had me worn-out entirely. I heard the knock again but didn't do anything other than turning my head to another side. The door was open; if someone needed something, they could straightway come in. My eyes snapped open as I heard my name along with the knock. It was Riya, I hastily rolled up and opened the door. Her upset face had me worried.

"Nitya. She was sleeping with me, and now she is not there," she swallowed as her eyes gleamed with tears she was holding back.

"She must be here only. Did you check the washroom?" I wore my slippers and rushed from one room to another room to look for Nitya. I checked my mother's room and found it empty.

"What time it is?" I asked, and Riya answered. It was around five in the morning. I sighed in relief.

"She is with my mother," I said and saw the muscles of her face relaxing a bit.

"Come with me," I said and took her to the Puja room. It was the time of the day my mother spent worshipping in the small temple we had at our home. Standing outside the room, we saw Nitya in my mother's lap as she explained something to Nitya about Lord Krishna. I looked at Riya and found her smiling in relief.

"I was worried that…" she didn't complete the sentence and closed her eyes.

"Don't worry, Riya, she is safe here," I appeased her.

"Yeah, sorry, I woke you up. I didn't know what else to do," she said, embarrassed.

"It's ok, Riya. I can understand as this place is new to you. Your worry was genuine. Do you want to go back to sleep? Don't worry about Nitya. She will be busy with my mother for another one hour," I said. Even though she went back to her room, but I knew she wouldn't breathe in relief until she had Nitya with her. I went back to sleep, and when I woke up next; I found all the three females in my house inside the kitchen. My mother was cooking the breakfast, and Riya was helping her, while Nitya just fussed that no one was letting her help. Picking her up in my lap, I nuzzled her stomach, and she burst out laughing.

"Would you like to play with me, Princess?" I asked, and she nodded with her mouth wide open in excitement. I laughed and nuzzled her one more time inhaling her delicious scent of baby powder. I blinked at Riya, telling her that I would take care of Nitya.

I brought her to the room where my mother kept my old toys, thinking that Nitya would find something interesting there to play, and I wasn't wrong. She picked up my small bat and asked to play cricket in the backyard. I was propelling the ball towards Nitya when my Phone started ringing. I smiled as I saw Ekta's name flashing on it. Holding the mobile precariously between my shoulder and ear, I took the call, "Hey,"

"Hello Mr Celebrity, We know that you are too busy, but do take out some time for us too," she jibed. I knew she was pulling my leg, because just two days before I had talked to her.

"There's nothing like that Ekta, and you know it," I answered as I jogged to pick up the ball.

"I know. I know. I was just kidding. Where are you by the way? In the gym?" she asked.

"No. I came to Dehradun yesterday," I replied as I threw the ball again to Nitya. She hit the six this time and started bouncing and screaming with happiness. I laughed seeing her this excited.

"Hey, what are you doing?" Ekta asked.

"Nothing. Just playing Cricket with Nitya," I answered, still laughing.

"Nitya?" she asked, and I suddenly realized I shouldn't have taken Nitya's name. But what harm she could cause!

"Hmm… Riya's daughter," I said as I again tossed the ball at Nitya.

"Riya. That hip…" she stopped mid-sentence. "What's she doing with you in Dehradun?" she asked, and I could picture her riled up, as her voice raised indicating her apparent dislike towards Riya.

"She is in trouble! Some problem with her husband and in-laws," Though I didn't want to, I replied, assuming that it would turn her a little considerate towards her.

"Wasn't that expected looking at her antics? We all knew she wasn't a family type girl," she hissed, and I heard my blood rushing to my ears. Why did she always become so judgmental when it came to Riya?

"Will you please stop being so rude to her? You know nothing about her," I yelled exasperated and noticed that Nitya was watching me. Closing my eyes, I tried to slacken my senses.

"Okay, okay, calm down," she said, and I sighed.

"Ekta, I don't know why are you so against her, but she is not a bad girl,"

"Okay," she whispered, and I knew I had hurt her.

"I am sorry, Ekta, for being rude," I apologized, holding the back of my neck.

"It's ok, Ady." She said, and after a pause, she added, "You like her. Don't you?" she asked, but I was no longer interested in talking anything to her about Riya.

"Bye, Ekta. Talk to you later," I clicked the call to end.

After breakfast, I headed to the *TingTong* office in Dehradun. It had been almost three months since I had been there. I met my branch manager and took all the details from him. The rest of the day was whirlwind of events. I was about to leave the office when the office boy came with another set of papers that needed my signatures. I took my time to go through the documents. It was regarding our deal with *The Kidzone*, a renowned playschool chain, for the supply of outdoor and indoor play equipment in all their branches. As I signed the papers, another idea flashed in my mind. I quickly dialled my manager's number.

"Mr Sharma, can you get outdoor play equipment installed in my backyard?"

"Umm…yes, sir," I knew he wanted to ask why, but being a new employee he couldn't.

"Tonight?" I asked.

"Umm... I will have to check the availability right now! I will inform you in five minutes,"

"Okay," I said and disconnected the call. Soon he confirmed that he would get it done that night only.

Nitya was fussing over something when I entered my home. Keeping my bag on the side, I took her in my arms. "What's wrong, Princess?" I asked. She curled her lower lip and looked at Riya angrily. I laughed, looking at her cute expressions.

"She is feeding me unhealthy food," Nitya carped.

"Banana is not unhealthy," Riya retorted.

"It is unhealthy. It has black marks on its skin. It has got a disease," Nitya snapped, and I couldn't help laughing aloud. I took the banana from Riya and peeled its skin.

"See, now it's perfectly healthy," I showed her the peeled off banana. She instantly brought her mouth near my ear and whispered which was not exactly a whisper, "I don't like bananas! Tell Mumma, it's unhealthy. Aren't we a team?" I stifled my smile and tried to look serious, and then whispered back in her ear, "If you finish this banana, you will get a surprise in the morning. A big surprise," I said. Astounded, her lips curved in perfect O.

"A big surprise. Really?" she asked, and I nodded my head in agreement. She clapped her hands joyously as I fed her the banana. She was truly heaven-sent; in such a short time, she had become a crucial part of my life. I couldn't even imagine my life without her. I couldn't understand how could her father not miss her? If I were he, I would have moved mountains to have her back in my life. And then it clicked me; maybe that's why he was after Riya. Perhaps he wanted Riya and Nitya back in his life, but Riya rebuffed. The thought made me twitchy. I wasn't ready to let them go. But these are just the speculations. I wouldn't know until I heard it from Riya herself. I was waiting for her to get settled here first so that she could tell me everything without any pressure. After dinner, I spent the next few hours in my music room, scribbling the lyrics and setting the melody of a song for my upcoming album.

CHAPTER 13

Down The Memory Lane

The amber sunshine burst through the curtain slits made me squint. Raising my head, I looked at the time, it was six in the morning. Turning on my stomach, I curled my arm around the pillow. I felt a feather-like tingling on my arm. When I opened my eyes, a wild curly head propped on hands greeted me with a warm smile. I laughed looking at her.

"What are you doing here, Princess?"

"Where is my surprise?" she asked.

"You got up this early for a surprise? Where is your mother?" I asked propping my head upon my palms, mirroring her.

"She is still sleeping, so I sneaked out,"

"Hmm... so you want your surprise? Wait for five minutes here. Let me freshen up," I said as I bolted up from the bed and rushed to washroom. Through the window inside, I looked at the backyard and found the castle-like play equipment with various rides standing in the center of the yard. When I came out, I found Nitya sitting in the same place. Tucking her tendrils behind her ear, she looked at me expectantly.

"Get a hair tie, Princess! Let me make your hair first," I said as I saw her struggling with the loose hair. She jumped from the bed and sprinted to her room. Holding a pink hair band in hand, she was back in a jiffy. I somehow managed to tie them in a messy pony and then took her in my arms as I headed towards the back door.

"Is the surprise backside?" she asked, wriggling her feet in my lap.

"Hmm... it was too big, couldn't fit inside," I said and saw her eyes widening looking at the Play Zone.

"I love you, Ady." She kissed my cheek and squirmed to get down. Once out of my grip, she rushed and climbed on it.

"Be careful, Nitya," I warned as I saw her climbing the steps hurriedly. I sat on the white cast iron bench on the corner and watched her sliding down. I had known her just for three days, and yet it seemed like she had always been with me. She was the clone of her mother: same curly hair, same big brown eyes and same smile that could warm any heart. I felt a commotion behind me, and when I looked back, I saw Riya coming towards me.

"It wasn't here yesterday. Did you bring it for Nitya?" she asked with her brow pinched, gesturing towards Nitya with her eyes. I bolted up as I tried to find the words. I felt like a kid who caught doing something without his parent's permission. I didn't know why I was afraid to tell her the truth.

"Umm... No, It was—" she cut me off holding a hand up and completed the sentence herself.

"A sample piece? For testing purpose?" she said in a stern voice, folding her arms to her chest. Scratching the back of my neck, I smiled feverously and bobbled my head.

"Do you realize, you are spoiling her?" she said, shaking her head. When I didn't answer and kept looking at her, she reprimanded, "I wouldn't be able to afford the things you are giving her, and one day she may hate me for this. So please stop pampering her,"

It did sting my heart. It felt like as if I had no right on Nitya. And what hurt more was that it wasn't a lie. Without mincing my words, I spurted, "I get it. She is your daughter, and I have no right on her. I will keep this in my mind." She threw her hands in exasperation as I pivoted to leave.

"I didn't mean that, Adyant," she yelled from behind, but I didn't look back and came to my room. I left early for the office that day. I needed time to get my head straight, and that wouldn't have happened around Riya and Nitya. I busied myself in work. After lunch, my manager handed me the papers of Employee contract that I had asked for Riya. She didn't need to fill all these forms, but I knew she wouldn't accept the job if I didn't treat her like a regular employee. After what happened in the morning, I was dubious that offering her a position here in Dehradun without asking her was a good idea. I squared the papers and kept them in a folder.

I reached my home around seven in the evening to find Riya apprehensively pacing here and there in the Drawing room. She was wringing her hands. The appalled look on her face had me worried. Alarms started beeping high in my head. I tossed my bag on the side table and rushed to her. Holding her shoulders, I looked into her eyes. She could never lie looking into the eyes. "What's wrong?" I asked, seeking an answer.

"Aunty. Talk to her," she said.

"What happened to her? And where is she?" I asked, looking towards the kitchen, her usual place at this time of the day.

"In her room. Please talk to her," she said anxiously. I nodded and gave her the papers those were still in my hand. "Read it and sign it," I said as I started to head to my mother's room.

"What are they?" she asked taking them from my hand.

“Employee contract form for *TingTong*,” I answered over my shoulder and rushed to my mother’s room.

I entered my mother’s room and saw her sitting on the edge of the bed. I instantly knew something was troubling her. I kneeled in front of her and held her hands.

“What’s wrong, Maa,” I asked, and she averted her eyes.

“How long is she going to stay here?” she asked me, rudely gesturing towards the door with her eyes. I understood she was asking about Riya.

“What happened? Did she do something wrong?” I asked, and she shook her head.

“Sudha came today,” she said, and I tried to connect the dots. I closed my eyes as I understood what was troubling her. Sudha aunty was Ekta’s mother.

“She told me everything about this girl’s character. I can’t believe you brought someone like her home,” she said, and I controlled the sudden surge of angst I felt for Ekta.

“That’s not true,” I tried to explain, but she cut me off.

“Her own parents have abandoned her, and now the in-laws. She is not our responsibility,” she yelled. It wasn’t my mother. I had no idea what all Sudha aunty had crammed in my mother’s head. I pressed my temples to gain the composure.

“She doesn’t have parents,” I said and saw the confusion etched on my mothers face. I told her everything that I knew about Riya. My mother listened to everything attentively, and as I finished, she had tears in her eyes. Now that was my mother. Always compassionate and caring.

“Oh, God!” her hand flew to her mouth.

“Yes. All I am saying is don’t listen to the people who don’t know her at all. She is in front of you, if you want, judge her from your own experience and not what other people say,” I said, and she nodded her head in acknowledgment.

"Did you say anything to her? She seemed upset when I came back," I asked.

"No, I didn't talk to her after that. But Sudha was rude to her," she said, and I nodded grinding my teeth. Telling Ekta about Riya being here was a mistake.

"Did she tell you what's the problem with her husband?" she asked and I shook my head.

"I didn't get enough time to ask her,"

"How are we suppose to help her if we don't know the problem?"

"I know! I have tried talking to her, but every time Nitya was around, and she doesn't want to talk about her husband in front of Nitya," I replied.

"I can understand that, talk to her now! I will take Nitya to temple with me," she said.

"I will! But I need to talk to someone else first," I said and got up. Through the back door, I came outside the house. I took out my phone from the pocket and pulled her number out. I sudden surge of anger oozed out of my body. I felt the blaze in my chest and tremble in my hand as I dialed Ekta's number.

"Hey Ady," she said in a cheerful voice. The bustle behind her told me that she was in some gathering, but I didn't care.

"Ekta, Will you please stop meddling in my life and start concentrating on your own damn life?" I spat through my gritted teeth.

"Ady, you are—" I stopped her mid-sentence.

"It's been six years, Ekta, since you married Nikhil. Get me out of your head and let me live here peacefully," I said and heard her breathing heavily. The commotion behind her hushed and I conjectured she came out of that gathering.

"Will you please listen to me?" she raised her voice this time, and I clenched my hands in anger.

"When is it going to get into the thick skull of yours that she is using you?" she yelled, and I could picture her pacing and gritting her teeth. A mirthless laugh escaped my lips before I said, "You have no idea, Ekta, how desperate I am to get used by her!"

I heard her groaning and then she was quiet. I wanted to disconnect the call, but I wanted this conversation over and done. After a few seconds that seemed like an eternity, she said, "You love her, Ady. Don't you?"

I froze listening to those words aloud. I could have dodged the question, but I didn't. Even though it felt wrong telling her before Riya.

"Yes, I do," A relief cascaded in my body as I admitted my feelings for her as if a war had ended within me. I heard her exhale loudly, and then there was silence.

"Why, Ady?" her voice trembled. When I didn't reply, she added, "Why her and not me?" I heard her sobbing. I knew I needed to comfort her, but suddenly, I felt short of words.

"If you go ask people around, I bet ninety-nine percent of them will approve me over her for you. Why can't you see that?" she sniffled.

"For God sake Ekta, you are married," I said pinching the bridge of my nose. "And she isn't?" she snapped, and I had to squeeze my eyes to contain my crossness.

"She has a kid too," she added. "Ever wondered Ady, why don't I have a child even after six years of my marriage?" she whispered after a hiatus, and I felt my breath hitched. Did she realize she was spoiling her life? Not only hers, but her husband's too? The silence was my only response. I couldn't think of anything that I could say to clear her mind. "Do you know how painful it is to be in unrequited love?" she asked as she cried. I laughed grimly on my own misery. Did I know how painful it was?

"Trust me, Ekta. I know it very well," I said and disconnected the call. I took a few minutes to myself to get the composure before entering the home. When I came inside my home, I saw Riya sitting on the chair perched at a corner. When she saw me coming, she stood up. "Adyant, I was waiting for you. I have read the contract papers, and I have also signed it," she said.

"Good. Do you still want to work from home?" I asked.

"Yes. And I was also thinking to search for a rental flat. Can you help me find one? You and Aunty have been kind enough to provide us space at the time of need, but I guess I should move out as I have a job now," she hesitated, and I did notice she didn't look at me when she said it. Before I could say anything, I saw my mother standing at her room's door.

"No one is going anywhere. This home is big enough to accommodate you two," she said, looking at Riya.

"Trust me, Aunty. It will be better for everyone. And it has nothing to do with what happened today," Riya said. Nitya came out of her room and wrapped her arms around Riya's leg. "Are we moving again, Mumma?" she asked, looking up at Riya with big tears in her eyes. "I like it here. I don't want to go. Can we stop playing this game?" she asked, and I felt the tightness in my chest. I kneeled, and took Nitya in my arms.

"You want to stay here?" I asked her, and she nodded as the tear rolled down her cheek. "Then no one is going anywhere," I said, and she enveloped my neck in her little arms.

"If you are so bent on this, you may pay me the rent," my mother said. It was evident that Riya wanted to reason, but she kept quiet. I let my mother handle this matter. She reached out for Riya. Holding her hand, she said, "I am sorry for today,"

Riya shook her head before saying, "But you didn't do or said anything wrong,"

"Neither did you, yet I thought bad about you. Please forgive me and stay here," my mother said, and Riya's lips curled up in half-smile.

"Nitya, do you want to come with me to the temple. I am sure, you will love it," My mother said looking at Nitya, who looked at Riya silently asking for her permission. Riya nodded, and Nitya jumped in ecstasy. She ran inside to wear her sandals and was back in a jiffy. She waved both of us bye as she left with my mother holding her finger.

"Don't worry. She is in safe hands," I said as I saw worry etched on Riya's face.

"I know. It's just I am not habitual of being without her," she said and then she smiled, "I don't know if I should be happy that she has started mingling with people other than me or sad that she didn't look twice back at me."

I smiled as I understood her dilemma. I reminded myself that I needed to talk to her. And before she took the conversation to somewhere else, I voiced my thought.

"Riya, can we talk?" I asked and saw the color of her face fading. It was good that she understood what we were going to talk about. She didn't say anything and kept looking at me as if pleading silently not to have this conversation. I sighed and took a few steps towards her. In a soothing voice, I said, "I need to know what I am dealing with. I can't help you if you don't tell me what's wrong," I looked at her for the response. She hesitated for a moment and then I saw the walls of indifference slowly climbing up. The stubborn side of her was back.

"You are dealing with nothing, Adyant. Stay out of my life. It's not something I can't handle myself. I have dealt with the worse before. Trust me. It's nothing. Just because I asked you for a favour, doesn't mean I am helpless," she said, quirking her brow up. I might not have spent much time with her, but I did know how to handle her resoluteness. I decided to change the topic for some time.

"Come with me," I said, taking another step towards her.

"Where?" she asked, confused.

"Don't ask. Just come," I said and held her elbow as I guided her to my favourite room upstairs—My music room. Equipped with all the latest musical instruments, it cost more than my entire home. The grey and black colored wall gave it a masculine look. The unevenly designed shelves on the front wall were all packed with the trophies I had won in the last few years. The adjacent wall was covered with all the certificates laminated and skillfully hanged along with the pictures of our memorable live concerts. She gasped as she entered and twirled on her heal for a quick view of the whole room. "Wow," she said, and a proud smile appeared on my face. She scrutinized everything in the room and then she looked at me as she said, "You have come a long way, Adyant. I am so proud of you." Hearing her say those words, I was tickled pink. She turned to look at the other wall that had the name of my band embossed with golden letters. She traced the letter 'R' with her finger as she said, "*Riyaz*... it means practicing music. Right? A lovely and apt name," she said and glanced at a few papers on the table where I had roughly scribbled the lyrics of our upcoming album the previous day.

"For everyone else, it means practicing music, but for me, it has a different meaning," I said as I rounded the table and stood in front of her.

"And what is that?" she asked. Without looking away from her, I reached down and fumbled to pick a marker from my table, and scribbled the meaning on whiteboard hanged in one of the walls.

Riya's

"This is how I look at this name," I said and saw her cheeks turning pink as the realization dawned on her.

"You kept your band name after me?" she asked, pointing the finger at her chest.

"Yes, I did," I replied honestly.

"But why?" she sounded exasperated, and I cringed at my big mouth.

"Because it wasn't possible if I hadn't met you that day," I said.

"Oh God! Adyant," she slapped her forehead and then shook her head. Standing in front of her, seeing her reaction, I felt like a kid being reprimanded.

"You are giving me credit more than I deserve. I did nothing! Nothing! I just talked. Something I did with every other boy in that marriage," she yelled and took a step towards me. Tugging on my suit jacket, she said, "If anyone deserves the credit, it's you! Your team! Your hard work. Your determination. I did absolutely nothing. You would have come off flying colors even without me because you were destined for this," her voice calm and compelling now. I breathed a laugh, and she looked at me, surprised.

"I was like that lost child who didn't know the way back home. You didn't just show me the right way, but also walked with me to safely drop me to my doorstep. It might be just the talking for you, but it was everything to me. You have no idea how uncertain and disheartened I was that time. You were the one who trusted me more than I trusted myself," I said. She looked down for a moment and then locked her eyes with mine. "I get it. I did feel the same way when I had met *Nana*," she said, and her eyes welled up. I took a step in her direction and clenched her shoulders, urging her to look at me.

"I know Riya, you are a strong girl, and I am sure you can handle this situation yourself, no matter how bad it is.

But I want to do something for you. Please let me in! If not for yourself then for me! Will you?" I said. She tried to avert her eyes, but I instantly cupped her face forcing her to look at me. "Say *yes,*" I ordered. She breathed out a laugh with her eyes fastened to mine. "Is that the only option?" she asked, and I nodded unable to bite back the smile that curved my lips at her comment.

"Oh shit! I forgot to apologize for today morning. I am really sorry. I didn't mean to hurt you," she said out of nowhere. I nodded pursing my lips, realizing that she was again trying to change the topic, but I didn't take the bait. Before she could take the conversation somewhere else, I dragged it back to the point.

"Can we now talk about what we really need to talk?" I said.

"Can we not have that conversation ever?" she retorted.

"Riya, I—" I tried to reason, but she stopped me.

"Please, I had had enough today. Let's do something exciting," she said with a glint in her eyes.

"Like what?"

"Like you sing your upcoming song for me," she said, gesturing the papers on the table, and I sniggered shaking my head. It was so difficult to get anything out of this girl if she didn't want to. But if she had mastered in tactfully changing the topic, I too was proficient in saying the things my way.

I closed my eyes and changed a few words of the song so that I may convey my message. Opening my eyes and I picked up my guitar. She sat on the chair in front of me. Leaning my back to the table, I strummed the chords and then started singing the song.

Nigahein wo sab keh jati hain,

Jo teri zubaan chhipati hai,

Main ek pal mein

haal-e-dil keh gya,

Tu kyun itna hichkichati hai

Jo mera sapna hai

kyu wo tera sapna nhi,

Jitna tu mera apna hai,

kyu utna main tera apna nhi...

I looked at her and found her looking at me the same way she had looked at me six years ago when I had sung the song for her. She quickly gathered her composure and shook her head.

"Is it just me who feel like you are singing to me? Or it happens with all of your listeners" she asked. I was about to answer that when the commotion downstairs caught our attention. Then first I heard Nitya crying and then my mother calling Riya's and me. Worried, we both rushed downstairs and found Nitya sitting on a chair with her knee covered in blood. I instantly kneeled to have a look at the wound while Riya said, "It's ok, baby girl. We will bandage it. It's nothing."

She went inside her room and came back with a small first-aid box. She bandaged Nitya whispering the comforting words in her ear that how brave she was, and how brave people get injured all the time. I smiled, looking at the two. It was so amazing to witness how a carefree and reckless girl once had turned into a caring and responsible mother. Once she finished bandaging her, I picked up Nitya in my arms and took her to her room. I heard my mother explaining how Nitya got injured while running and playing with other kids in the temple. I came inside the room and found Riya's handbag open and hastily thrown at the side of the bed. I shoved it to the other side to make space for Nitya while I noticed something peeping out of the bag. I made Nitya lie on her back and rounded the bed to have a more precise look at it. It couldn't be what it looked like! A closer look made my blood run cold as I realized I wasn't wrong. I took it out of her bag and held it in my hand.

A fully loaded Pistol.

I exhaled through my mouth, trying to get my heartbeat back in rhythm. Riya entered the room and froze seeing me holding her Pistol. Before I could ask her anything, she looked at Nitya and said, "You are a brave girl, Nitya. No need to lie down here. Go outside and play." Nitya picked up her doll and looked at Riya. "My doll is injured too. Can I bandage her?" she asked, looking at the first aid box in Riya's hand. She took out a pack of Band-Aid and gave it to Nitya, who sprinted out of the room. Riya warily padded towards me and took the Pistol from my hand. Picking her bag from the bed where I had left it open, she sauntered towards the almirah. She kept the gun back in her purse and stuffed it inside the almirah. She stood there with her back to my side as she closed the door. I knew she was preparing herself to answer. I walked to her and clenched her shoulder, forcing her to look in my direction. She turned with her eyes still looking down.

"Please tell me you haven't murdered someone," I said, and she laughed nervously.

"No! Not yet," she answered, and my eyebrows touched the hairline.

"Not yet?" I asked astounded. "Well! We need to have this conversation in detail," I said it with firmness in my voice, not giving her any chance to recoil.

"Do you have a license for it?" I asked, and my eyes popped out when she shook her head. "It's stolen," she answered.

Shit! She was carrying a fully loaded stolen gun all the time. She could have got caught—We could have got caught. I wasn't the one to support the lawbreaking. For someone who had never broken a traffic rule, this all was huge.

"You know just a few minutes before, I appreciated you in my head that how impeccably you have turned into a responsible mother, but now..." I shook my head thwarted with her actions.

"Yogit Pradhan. He is my husband," she said.

Yogit Pradhan, I reiterated this name in my head, and my eyes widened in shock as recognition dawned on me.

"Elder son of Devendra Pradhan? The politician?" I asked, and she nodded. A family of goons turned politician long back. Devendra Pradhan was the president of the Jan Seva Party. He had served as Cabinet Minister too. In the upcoming legislative assembly elections, he was projecting his son, Yogit Pradhan, as a candidate for the chief minister. As per the news, speculations were that Yogit Pradhan was getting married to the daughter of a former minister for their political alliance, and also that if this marriage happened, this coalition would definitely come in power. I didn't know much about them, but I had heard a lot of not-so-good things about the family. Riya might have noticed the horror on my face as she said, "Yeah, it's that bad,"

I closed my eyes and rubbed my hands on my face before saying, "Shit! Riya, what you have gotten yourself into?"

"I know, Adyant. That's why I wanted to keep you away from all this. But it's not late, either. I will move out of your place as soon as possible," she said, misunderstanding my words.

"Are you insane?" I sputtered, raising my voice.

"I am not worried about me, Riya! I am worried about you,"

"Don't be! I will handle it," she said, and I pressed my temples in frustration.

"How?" I snapped.

"I have collected proofs of the scams and other things they are involved in. If need be, I may use it against them. They are not cogent evidence, but if someone could dig deep, they could surely provide the right direction for the investigation. I may blackmail him," she said, and I couldn't help groan that escaped my lips.

"Kill me, please," I said exasperated. She couldn't be so naïve to think that she could fight them with some inconsequential proofs! "Do you have any idea how powerful they people are? We are nothing more than an ant in front of them," I said.

"I do know! I have spent several years with him," she said, and her eyes welled up. I turned to look away from her momentarily and closed my eyes. "Is he after you because of what you have against him?" I asked. She looked down, wringing her hands. I sensed that there was more in the story. And it had to be if she bothered to carry a gun for her protection. Taking a few deep breaths, I pivoted to look at her. "We need to inform this to police," I said. My hand reflexively went to my phone to call Chauhan uncle. He could show us the right way. I was about to dial when Riya held my hand to stop me.

"No! No police, please," she said. I froze as I saw her stricken face.

"I am going to tell Maa to look after Nitya, and then we are going to talk. Meet me in music room upstairs in five minutes," I ordered, and she nodded in response looking down.

CHAPTER 14

Down The Memory Lane

"I was in the first year of my graduation, when I saw Yogit for the first time, and had an instant crush on him. He was in the final year then," she laughed humorlessly. We were in the music room. She was sitting on the chair while I leaned against the wall. "He was sturdy, rough and cocky, there was nothing decent about him, but I liked him. It was his farewell when, for the first time, he noticed me. We chatted for sometime and exchanged number," she said. I would be lying if I said it didn't hit me like a punch that she never exchanged her number with me. Knowing that someone didn't reciprocate your love is one thing, but listening to them how they responded to someone else's is like a blow in the gut.

"For a long time, we were in touch with each other through the phone. Then we started meeting. Love blossomed. I was in my final year when I found out that... that I was pregnant. I was about to graduate and had a job in my hand. It was all unexpected. We mutually decided to terminate it, but when it was the day, I couldn't." she looked up at me and added, "Wouldn't that have made me worse than my own parents? They at least, gave me birth." She didn't need my validation, but her eyes darted at me, silently asking if she did the right thing. When I nodded, she continued, "Yogit supported me in my decision, and within a week we were legally married. Yogit insisted on hiding this marriage and laying low. We bought a flat together. Being pregnant, I started working freelance. Yogit helped me to get the business. I had everything, life felt dreamlike. He didn't tell his parents even after Nitya was born. He said it would affect his father's image, and I understood. Things were going fine till Nitya was two. He didn't live with us, but he kept visiting us almost daily. And I was fine with it. How could I have doubted him? He used to tell me everything. His good deeds and also his bad deeds. How they got rid of someone trying to expose them? Their scams and everything. Don't all these things scream that he trusted me more than anyone? I had no reason to doubt him. One day he told me that the party has decided to project him in the upcoming elections. That was the wake-up call for me. I knew that if he didn't accept me in front of everyone now, he would never be able to. Once you are a public figure, everything hidden becomes the sin. I didn't want to be his dirty secret.

"Moreover, Nitya's future was in question. I insisted on to talk to his family, and he listened. In one month, we both were at his parent's house. They let me live in but didn't accept me. Neither Nitya. They gave us a separate one room set outside the main house. I didn't argue. Wasn't that my chance to prove how determined I was for my dream?" I recalled her words regarding her dream—*to have a family.* "I knew it would take time for them to accept the fact that their son had married someone without their consent. I did everything to please them. But once someone has decided not to like you, no matter what you do, it will never be enough. They didn't let Nitya and me enter the main house, saying that they don't know my religion, my caste, and they will let me in after the sanctification. I lived there for more than a year, and with every passing day, I saw Yogit slowly drifting away from us. He stopped seeing us daily citing that he was busy in campaigning. He started sleeping in his own room inside the main house, leaving us two in that servant-quarter. Perhaps his parents had brainwashed him, but I don't blame them. If Yogit truly loved us, he wouldn't have strayed. I knew things were getting out of my hand, but what else I could have done except waiting for him to realize. One day I heard a rumor regarding his wedding for a political alliance. That was the final nail in the coffin. Without caring about their order not to enter the house, I went in. Surprisingly there was no one. As I headed further, I heard his voice. I peeped in the room and found three to four people discussing how to get rid of my daughter and me. I still remember his father's exact words. He said to Yogit that he needed to get rid of the garbage he had brought in with him. What hurt me most was he didn't even flinch on his father's words," she said and closed her eyes momentarily.

"You were his legally wedded wife. Wasn't you?" I asked. She could have easily proved that in the court.

"Yogit too said the same thing to his father. To which he replied it could be taken care of. His father also asked him who could come looking for us—Nitya and me, if both of us get disappeared. His answer was 'No one.'" Closing her eyes, she inhaled sharply to collect herself. I knew she was trying hard to keep her tears in check.

"Now, as I knew their intentions, I had to act fast, but I couldn't leave without retaliating. I knew this meeting would take time. So I took the risk and instantly rushed to his room and got hold on his laptop.

"Thankfully, He hadn't changed his password. I knew where he used to keep all the critical information on his laptop. I attached all of them and emailed them to me, and I also took his pistol from the almirah. He had taught me to shoot. Who had known then that one day, I would use this skill to protect myself from him! I didn't pack much stuff except some cash, jewelry and a few clothes that could fit in my handbag. I left that home saying that I was going to the doctor. Otherwise, they wouldn't have allowed me out," she paused, and I sighed.

"Thank god, he doesn't know you have proofs against him," I said and saw her hesitantly looking here and there.

"Don't tell me, Riya, that you have already blackmailed him?" I asked, and she looked down, wringing her hands.

"I had no place where I could run, so I went to the police. It seemed the right choice then. I told them that I have proofs to expose that family, thinking that being the witness they would have to protect me. They sent me to a room and told me to wait there. Nitya was getting cranky, so I took her outside. They sent a lady constable with me. She too was a new mother and perhaps seeing me with Nitya had molten her heart. She told me to run, and also that my in-laws would be arriving anytime—police had informed them. I was clueless about what to do next. Where to go? That kind lady gave me an address in Delhi and told me to meet her relative, who would get me a place to crash in. This is how I reached Delhi. I went to that address and met this kind person. Not only a place to live, but he also helped me to get a job in that restaurant. Otherwise, who would have employed me without the credentials and with a fake identity," she completed and sighed. And that explained why I couldn't find her in the restaurant. She had faked her identity.

"That lady constable might have given your location to them," I said contemplating.

"Maybe! I hope they hadn't done anything bad to her," she whispered.

"Your father. Didn't he help you?" I asked. Of course, he wouldn't have helped her willingly, but maybe because of the hold, *Nana* had over him.

"I stopped bothering him the moment I started earning. I never turned to him, neither he did try to reach me," she answered.

"And *Nana*?" I asked. If she had someone to guide her, then she wouldn't have spent the nights alone dreading the worse.

"He died two years ago," she said, and I inhaled sharply. I kept looking at her while she gazed down. She was brave. Despite having such terrible experiences,

she never let it reflect on her face.

"Don't look at me that way," she said, sensing my gaze on her. Then she covered her face with her hands in embarrassment. "What you will think about me! Every time I meet you, I have a horrible story to tell," she said, and a slow laugh escaped my lips.

"I must say Riya, you are brave," I said honestly.

"Last I remember, Brave wasn't the synonym of stupid," she said, and I laughed.

I asked some more questions about her post-wedding life, and she answered all of them. We left the things hanging, as we both had no idea how to go about this. I needed some time to contemplate before I could reach to the conclusion.

I was in my room when I opened my laptop and searched for Yogit Pradhan. I had heard his name in the news but never cared to look carefully at him. The search engine showed several results. I clicked on his image. He looked robust with a tall, masculine body and raucous personality in the picture. I typed 'Yogit Pradhan's wife', and it showed the same news regarding him getting married for political alliance. Not a single page linked his name with Riya or talked about his daughter. Then I clicked on the video of his latest rally and found his speech for the hundreds of supporters sitting in front of him. My muscle tightened looking at his images. My stomach roiled thinking Riya chose him and not me. *You have much more fans than him, Ady. No need to get jealous.* A scorn-filled laugh escaped my lips as I reminded myself this.

CHAPTER 15

Down The Memory Lane

"Ady, get me down," Nitya shrieked as she wriggled her legs sitting on the child carriage on the shopping cart. I loved the sound when she called me by my name. It was Sunday morning, and I had brought Riya and Nitya to the supermarket. Riya wanted to purchase some woolens for Nitya and herself. Riya was checking out the rows in kid's section, while I followed her, wheeling the cart and looking after Nitya.

"Nitya, keep quiet," Riya chastised Nitya keeping a finger on her mouth.

"Adyant, you really don't have to stay here. I will manage," Riya said, gazing at me.

"It's ok! I like shopping," I replied with a crooked smile on my face.

"Why do I remember someone saying that he hated shopping? Wasn't that you?" she said, ticking her finger on her temple feigning to think.

"Well! That was me, but then I got a chance to spend some time with a great shopping connoisseur, and I started loving it," I said, smiling facetiously at her. She shook her head and disappeared in another row stocked with clothes.

"Ady, get me down," Nitya whisper shouted this time.

"Why?" I asked.

"You are so stupid. It's my shopping. I want to choose clothes for me," she reprimanded me. What was wrong with both of the girls? They both scolded me as if I was younger to them.

"Okay, Princess," I capitulated and helped her to get down. She ran to the row stocked with gowns and picked up a long blue princess dress. Holding it up in her hands, she rushed to her mother. "Mumma, buy me this, please," she requested.

"No, Nitya. We are here to buy winter wears," she said and hanged the gown back. "See, I got this for you," Riya said as she sized the sweater holding it to Nitya's shoulders. Once satisfied, she put the sweater in her basket. I saw Nitya's face falling with the displeasure as she looked at me. Without caring about Riya, I picked the same gown and put it in my cart. "Whatever you want, Princess, put it here. No need to bother your mother." She smiled and ran from one row to another, looking for the things for her. She picked up an oversized top and dropped it in the cart. "It's not your size, Princess," I told her.

"I will wear it when I grow up," she said without caring to look at me. Soon my cart was filled to its brim with clothes, sandals, toys, chocolates, and what not. I saw that little creature running back to me, and I couldn't hold my laugh as she hastily threw the hair clips in the already full cart.

"Mumma is coming. What are we going to do now?" she whisper-shouted at me. And it had me anxious because I had no idea how I was going to persuade Riya to pay for it all. But one thing was sure I wouldn't let that little heart break. Riya came to our side and eyed the shopping cart in my hand. She looked at me first, and then shaking her head, she averted her eyes towards Nitya. "We are not buying any of it," she said sternly to Nitya who looked at me expectantly.

"Well! I am paying for everything," I said, and Riya snapped her eyes at me.

"You are paying for nothing, Adyant. Stay out of it," she warned. She looked like an annoyed lioness that moment, and I had heard somewhere that if you look into the eyes of a lioness without blinking, she won't attack you. I looked into her eyes but burst out laughing as I thought about the analogy.

"Okay. Do you want me to pay for your stuff?" I asked, gesturing to her basket.

"No," she said firmly.

"Princess, do you want me to pay for your stuff?" I asked Nitya but kept my eyes fastened to Riya. Nitya nodded her head in *yes*.

"So the decision is made. I am paying for her stuff but not yours," I said, and Riya rolled her eyes.

"You are spoiling her," she reiterated.

"Then let me, please. Do you ever think that maybe it's you… you both, who are spoiling me? I may get used to all this, and one day, you will push me away. The same way you did years ago," I said and immediately regretted my words. She turned and strolled towards the billing section. She paid for her stuff and didn't say a word when I paid for Nitya's. The drive back to home was quiet as Nitya slept on the back seat while Riya gazed outside sitting on the passenger seat. As we reached home, the rest of the day blurred fast.

Riya and I were making the arrangements for the dinner in the kitchen when my mother switched the channel from cartoons to the news. We didn't talk much after our argument in supermarket and avoided bumping to each other. I didn't know what was going in her head and why she was behaving that way, but I did realize that I had to make an effort to clear the air, that's why I deliberately offered to help in the kitchen and told Maa to sit with Nitya. Riya was transferring the cooked lentil in the serving bowl when I took a step towards her to make conversation. I was about to say something when we both heard Nitya shrieking 'Dedda', and I saw Riya freeze. Nitya again said the same word and Riya rushed out dropping the specula. It clattered as it fell on the floor. I too followed her to see what made her react that way. She was standing in the middle of the drawing-room. Her eyes clapped on the TV screen as it displayed the news showing Yogit's face. My mother looked back and forth between Riya and me. I was yet to tell my mother what all Riya had told me about her husband. I gestured her to calm down and that I would fill her later.

"This was our reported outside the hotel where the Pradhan family was spotted this evening. Speculations are that they have assembled for engagement of Yogit Pradhan with Swastika Parihar. We are yet to get confirmation from the reliable sources. As soon as we get the confirmation, we will bring it to our audience. Till then, keep watching."

The news anchor said, and then a health drink commercial took over the screen. I picked up the TV remote and turned it off. Riya pivoted to glance at me. That one look on her face said so much. I saw her breaking within, I saw her shattering with every breath, but she didn't say anything. She turned to look at Nitya, and a smile curved her lips. She picked her up and hugged her tight. I did notice she didn't eat dinner properly and took off early for the bed. I wanted to talk to her, to soothe her but I couldn't. She was the woman who loved to fight her own battles, so I gave her time to contemplate.

Lying on my bed, I kept thinking about her reaction to the news. She concealed everything within. Someone who didn't know her well would consider her emotionless, but I saw the damage in those eyes. I saw the vulnerability veiled in the smile that she gave to Nitya. I saw her seeking strength when she picked up and hugged Nitya.

I rolled out of bed to check on her. I went outside her room and saw the door ajar. Though lights were off, I was damn sure she wasn't sleeping. So many times, I lifted my hand to knock at the door and brought it back. Clenching my fist, I had just turned to leave when I saw the back door open. As I sprang out to the backyard, I saw a figure curled on the bench. I padded towards her. She had wrapped herself in a blanket. Her feet propped up on the bench and head buried in knees. She didn't even notice sitting me beside her.

"You okay?" I asked, and she snapped up her gaze, astounded to find me there.

"Yeah," she said and turned her head to the opposite side.

"Planning to retaliate?" I asked to make the moment lighter. She laughed as she lifted her head and looked at me. A tendril escaped from her ponytail and teased her face as the cool breeze wafted. I fisted my hands to stop myself from reaching out to remove it from her face. She might have guessed my intentions as she did it herself.

"I need to move out from here, Adyant. I can't stay here and put you and aunty in danger," she said, offering a side of her blanket. I took it and pulled it around my upper body. Was that what she worried about? Our safety?

"And I can't let you fight alone knowing it's dangerous," I said, locking my eyes with her.

"You don't have to, Adyant. You have already done a lot for us," she said.

"You and Nitya are my responsibility now," she started to say something, but I held up my hand, telling her to let me complete first. "I am not letting you go, Riya, no matter how dangerous it is. Aren't we a team?" I smiled as I repeated Nitya's words. "I don't know how it happened, Riya, but you both have become an integral part of me. I can't sleep peacefully here knowing that you both are struggling alone somewhere. We all are together in this now," I completed.

"You don't realize the risk you are taking, Adyant. Trust me, I am not worth it," she said glancing at me.

"Does a diamond ever know how precious it is? You have no idea how worthy you are!" I said. She leaned her head on the back of the bench and closed her eyes. I mirrored her gesture and focused on the sky above us, where the clouds had partially veiled the moon. Did it lessen the beauty of the moon? Not in the least—Instead, it made the view breathtaking. Amber moon rays fighting the dark clouds and making them appear silver. Difficulties never make us worthless; rather it makes us shine even more. Then why did she think that what she went through before made her any lesser? In my opinion, she was better than this moon, because she gleamed with her own light, not the borrowed one.

"It's a moot point considering everyone who had me has already thrown me out of their lives," she said with her eyes still closed, hauling me out of my trance.

"Because they are nescient, they threw the diamond away, thinking it was a stone." My reply was quick. I looked in her direction as I heard a closemouthed laugh escaping her lips.

"What?" I asked.

"Adyant Lohani, I am a married woman and a mother too. These lines are getting you nowhere," she said, looking at me with just one eye open, and pursed lips as she tried to bite back the smile.

"Ah! I am hurt," I held my hand to my heart in false pain and feigned a scowl. "It's a shame that my lines couldn't hit the target. Otherwise, you have no idea how these lines have gotten me a huge female fan following," I said and heard her laughing holding the belly.

"Seriously, but I want to know why don't you have anyone in your life yet?" she asked, wiping the tears of a laugh from corner of her eyes. I shrugged in response, but when she raised her brows, indicating she wanted the answer. I responded honestly.

"Let's just say, I haven't found someone yet," I said, and she rolled her eyes.

"I don't believe that. You are smart, successful and too good-looking. How is it even possible that you didn't find someone?" she said, and I shook my head, snorting out a laugh.

"Good-looking?"

"Yes! You are, just look at you—" She tilted on her seat abruptly giving me her full attention. Her eyes wandered over my face as she added, "Expressive eyes, radiant face, chiseled features, and the stubble." I lowered my gaze to her mouth as her tongue came out to wet her lips. She fought the smile that tried to curve her lips and almost won. Was she flirting with me?

"You have a personality to die for. And God! You sing so well," she said, holding her hand to her chest facetiously. I couldn't help the blush that reddened my face at her detailed and frisky praise. I pretended to rub my face to mask it.

"Well! Thank you. But I really didn't find anyone. Call me an old schooler, but I am not the one to fool around someone for fun. If I get myself into a relationship, I will make it last forever," I said.

"The way you write your songs, it's hard to believe that you have never been in love," she said, and I nodded understanding her well.

"I did love someone. Long back. But she preferred someone with a gun than the guitar, and left me heartbroken," I scrunched my nose teasingly and heard her exhaling a laugh.

"And now they both are playing gun-gun, and you are playing the guitar in between," she laughed at her joke making me smile too. She was the only one who could make fun out of a terrible situation. I wondered how life would have been different for both of us if that day she had given me her number; If she hadn't pushed me away; If I had fought a little more for her; If she had called me as per her promise. There were so many *ifs*, but no answers.

"Sometimes I wonder what life would have been if the things had ended differently between us," she said, and I smiled realizing that it wasn't only me playing the *ifs* in my mind.

"I was wondering the same thing," I said, leaning back and looking up at the sky.

"Tell me, what would we have been doing right now then?" she asked, mirroring my gesture and looking up.

"I don't know. Maybe sitting on the same bench, talking or planning about something,"

"Why am I at your home? Are we married?" she asked, and I found myself at the loss of words momentarily. I didn't know what she was expecting, but I clung to the future I had envisioned for both of us. I looked down first and then at her. Resting her head on the top of her knees, she locked her eyes with mine.

"Yes. Long back. I had proposed you after our first gig," I said, and she inhaled sharply before unfolding herself and looking up again. I didn't know how she was going to take it, so to make the moment light I added, "But you were too adamant. You took more than a week to answer me and made me do so many things to woo you,"

"That's quite possible," she said and laughed.

"Tell me, sitting here what we are planning about?"

"We are planning a vacation," I said, and she turned to me all excited. Though she never admitted, I knew she was a passionate traveler.

"Vacation?" she confirmed.

"Yeah. To oceans, deserts, and mountains," I said, and she smiled regaining her previous position.

"You remember? Tell me, where are we going then?" she said, gazing up and smiling softly.

"There is a problem, and we are arguing right now," I teased.

"Really? Why?" she asked, gazing at me.

"You want desert, and I want beaches," I pursed my lips in false disappointment.

"Why not mountains?" she asked, arching her brows.

"We have already been there before Nitya was born. But now we decided not to go there as Nitya is too young now and might get cold,"

"Is Nitya there too?" she asked, and I saw her smile widening.

"Who named her?"

"Me,"

"Then she is there," I said, returning her smile.

"What did we decide then?" she again looked up at the sky.

"Dubai, as we get to see the desert as well as the beaches,"

"When will we go to the mountains then? After five years?"

"No! Because then we are going to have two more young kids," I smiled envisioning the future that could have been ours.

"Two more? How many kids do you want?" she asked snickering.

"At least three! One to look after my dad's business, one to take my place in the band and one just in case if one of them chooses to do something different,"

"Some farsighted you are!" she said, clapping her hands mockingly. I laughed.

"Do you know what we are doing twenty years later from now?" she said, and I looked at her.

"You are pacing angrily in the drawing-room, and I am looking at you," she said with a sly smile on her face.

"And why I am angry?" I asked with my brows pinched in confusion.

"Nitya. She is in love with a boy you don't like. And she wants to marry him," she said, stifling a smile. I didn't find anything amusing in it; instead, I felt my jaw tightening.

"Shit! You think hiring goons will help in this case?" I said, and she burst out laughing.

"I knew it," she slapped my shoulder laughing and I couldn't help laughing with her.

"No. Seriously, but I am not letting her marry if I don't like the boy," I said.

"As if she is going to ask for your approval," she laughed, wiping the corners of her eyes. "She will. Because she loves me more than him," I didn't know from where I got the confidence to punch that line, but somewhere in my heart, I knew I was true.

"Aren't you awfully confident?" her shoulders shook slightly as she chuckled. The gloss in her eyes drew my attention to her. But before I could conjecture the emotion behind them, she hastily wiped the moisture from her eyes. Leaning back, she again glanced up the sky. I didn't know how much time passed, but she kept looking at the sky without a blink as if stars were soothing her inner turmoil. She appeared so divine in the silver moonlight. I kept looking at the side of her face as she slowly closed her eyes. Her each and every feature was etched in my mind, yet I couldn't touch her when she was just a few inches away from me. I had felt the warmth of her memories, yet when she was in front of me, I couldn't feel her. I saw a teardrop escaping the edge of her eyes. I saw the movement of her neck as she swallowed the emotions. I saw her nose flared as the first sob escaped her lips. I felt the tremble in her body as she let her guards down and bared her vulnerable side. And then she let the emotions she had been warring inside her since the past few weeks wash over her. I did hear what she said next that scratched my soul and left me wounded for my entire life.

"I loved him, Adyant. I really really loved him," she wailed, and I instantly wrapped my arm around her shoulder. "He made my dream come true. I had finally found a family with him. My heart can't accept the fact that he never loved me. He wouldn't have married me if it weren't for love. The hunger of power has blinded him so much that he can't see how badly he is hurting me. His passion has overweighed my love. What am I suppose to do now?" she cried and brought her knees to her chest. She sobbed, and I let her pour out all the emotions that were troubling her. After a hiatus, she added, "Why does life feel like sand sometimes, Adyant? The more I tighten up my fist, the faster it seems to slip out of my grip," she said, and I ran my hand up and down her arm to appease her.

"Sitting with you here and talking about *what-ifs*, every second, I felt like I was cheating on him. My conscience kept bringing his face in front of me. Did he feel the same way when he put the ring on her finger today? Did he think about me when he promised her a forever? A promise he wouldn't be able to break ever. Did he realize that if one day he decides to come back to me, he wouldn't be able to, because it won't be easy for him to get rid of her as easily as he thought in my case? There are people, who would look for her," I could hear the hysteria as she voiced her fear. Was she expecting him to come back to her? The thought was painful, but I didn't have time to process it as she continued, "Did he think about his little girl who every night asks me about her *Dedda*?" Her body shook, and I held her tightly, even though I felt used. The future that I had just envisioned with her, she was never a part of it. Did she realize that she just took me to heaven and then dropped me down to die? I had considered that she saw Yogit as her mistake hitherto. It was painful to know that she actually loved him. And what hurt more was she used me to secretly punish him for his infidelity. Did she realize that she had also punished me? And for what? But I didn't say it aloud. She was hurt and broken, and she needed me. And that was the only thing that mattered. I would shed the last drop of my blood if that could take away her pain.

"Why do people lie, Adyant? Don't they know how much it hurts? You know, what he used to say? That I am his strength. His breath of fresh air and one day, he wanted to get rid of me. I trusted him. Why did he do this to me? Wasn't my love strong enough? Wasn't my love true?" She added.

"No love is true, Riya. There always is a little selfishness hidden in it, and neither it is strong. It's like a fragile thread that could be broken just by a single tug. It looks strong when the two people holding the ends are strong and determined to make it last forever. It looks true when the two people in love are true to each other. It takes two to last it forever," I said, looking up at the sky.

"You are right. We broke the thread of our love by moving apart. At least I wasn't the first to move away," she said, resting her head on her knees. "Sometimes, I wish if I could blur everything around me, and lose myself in the oblivion. But then I realize, feeling this way is also a kind of blessing. It makes me feel alive. Dead people don't feel pain and hurt. Do they?" she asked without expecting an answer. I kept running my hand up and down to soothe her while she rested her head on my shoulder. I was no longer sure who was consoling whom. We both were hurt. We both were broken in a way.

She because of him.

I because of her.

CHAPTER 16

Down The Memory Lane

I ran my hand over the blue silk Kurta to straighten it as I stood up after praying in the temple. I came out with my mother and saw Nitya playing in the verandah outside the temple with her new friends. I did believe in God, but I wasn't the one to visit temples regularly. My mother had a routine to come here twice a day— morning and evening. And now Nitya too accompanied her. But that day I had to go with her. It was my birthday, and it didn't matter that I was turning twenty-eight, my mother still insisted on celebrating my birthday as we had been doing since I was born—First the puja in the temple and then visit an orphanage. I let her do it her way because all I wanted was she to be happy and satisfied. I watched as Nitya sat on a platform, while her friend narrated her some story animatedly. I saw her cute face scowling at something her friend had said. I had an urge to go to her and see if she was upset about something, but then I remembered what Riya had told me the other day.

'Don't rush to her every time you see her in trouble. Let her handle the situation herself. She should learn to get up herself every time she falls. This is how she will learn to stand up for herself.'

Well! Screw that.

Nitya curled her lower lip as the other girls laughed at her. And that was it. I could no longer stop myself. Riya wasn't here, and she would never know how I handled this situation. I padded to her and picked her up in my lap. I glared at her friends who were a little elder than Nitya. "Why you all are laughing at her?" I asked.

"She has never seen snow," one of the girls giggled.

"Princess, didn't you tell them that we are going to Mussoorie this weekend?" I said with a smile. Dumbfounded, she looked at me with her big brown eyes full of hope.

"Do we have snow there?" she asked, and I nodded my head. "A lot of snow, and also we are going to make the biggest snowman ever there?"

"Really? Yay… we are going to Moori," she clapped her hand elatedly, and I laughed.

The whole way back to the home, she kept asking me about the Mussoorie pronouncing it Moori. Walking beside me, my mother tried to teach her to pronounce it correctly, but she couldn't. Riya hadn't come with us and offered to make breakfast at home. As each step made us closer to home, I started to worry how was I going to explain this Mussoorie thing to her. As soon as we entered, Nitya rushed to Riya, bouncing and jumping. "Mumma, we are going to Moori," she exclaimed hugging Riya's legs. "Moori?" she looked at me for an answer, and I shrugged in response. "Yay… Moori. We have a lot of snow there," Nitya explained, stretching her arms wide to indicate *a lot of snow*. Riya looked puzzled as she darted her gaze from me to my mother.

"She is talking about Mussoorie. Ady just promised her a trip there," my mother elucidated, and I closed my eyes preparing myself for a lecture that how I was spoiling Nitya.

"Really? What happened to *Nitya is too young, and we can't go to the mountains*? And that she may catch a cold?" she scoffed quirking her brow at me.

"Umm…That was for vacation. We aren't going on vacation. We will go there, touch the snow and come back," I said, and Nitya chimed in, "And we gonna make the biggest snowman ever,"

"Yeah, that too," I nodded in agreement. Both of us looked at Riya, and she just shook her head and said nothing.

Thank god! I sighed.

"We also have a birthday party in the evening. You will get to play a lot of games," my mother said to Nitya.

"Birthday Party?" Riya Asked.

"Not exactly Birthday party, but we go to an orphanage to share our happiness with the kids," my mother said, and I noticed her body getting tensed momentarily. That reminded me that she never liked people celebrating birthdays in an orphanage. But soon she recovered and smiled.

"Shall we have breakfast now? I cooked Chhole-Puri," Riya said, turning to the kitchen. Everything seemed so real as if it had always been like this—Riya preparing us the breakfast, while Nitya playing with my mother. A real happy family. I could get used to it.

In the evening, when we all were ready to go, Riya came with an excuse that she would stay at home and prepare us dinner. I didn't want to force her, but my mother insisted her to come along, and she couldn't negate. She wore blue jeans with the jacket that we had bought from the supermarket the other day. Nitya wore her princess gown. I did notice Riya anxious when I parked the car outside the Orphanage. I hoped not to disappoint her as we entered, all the kids dressed in new dresses cheered as we emerged in. The open yard was decorated with the balloons, and a large table in the center covered with white satin cloth had massive cake on it.

Nitya instantly ran to the inflatable slide-and-bounce Play Park perched at one corner. She quickly mingled with the other kids and started playing with them. Soon we started the celebration, but I wasn't the one to cut the cake. The birthday song wasn't warbled for me. There were lots of hugs and kisses, but I wasn't the one to receive them. There were a lot of birthday gifts, but none of them was for me because we were there to celebrate those kids' birthday that had no one to make their day special. Something I had started after pondering upon what Riya had told that guy once. My chest gushed with the delight as I saw Riya easing up and becoming part of the celebration. She played musical chair with the kids and literally stomped her feet when she was out. She also got her arm temporarily tattooed with a dragon. She watched the magic show sitting on the ground with other kids. Standing on a corner, I watched her asking riddles to kids and laughing on her own stupid jokes. I watched her dancing with the kids as they tried to copy her moves. She caught my eye, and I saw her glowing with the contentment. She gestured me to come and join them, and I just shook my head. I was more than gratified seeing the girl I had lost long ago. She smiled and threw a flying kiss at me, making me laugh wistfully. It seemed like I was transported to six years back when I had fallen in love with this imperfectly perfect girl. So much had changed. I had wished her to be happy, and my heart cringed thinking that she never got the love she deserved.

We drove back home in silence — all too tired. Nitya slept holding a bundle of balloons on the backside with Riya, while my mother sat beside me. As I parked the car, Riya tried to pick Nitya, but she couldn't as Nitya never lose hold on the balloons. We laughed at her. I carefully picked Nitya and took her to the room. After tucking her in her bed, I kissed her forehead. I snickered as she was still holding balloons tight in her hand. As I stood up to leave, I saw Riya standing on the door glancing at me. I held her gaze as she slowly took a step towards me. My brows furrowed as I tried to surmise what was going in her mind. She slowly closed the distance and snaked her arms around my waist. Resting her head on my chest, she hugged me. It felt like as if the universe had stilled to witness this moment. I couldn't move, I couldn't breathe, too scared that this moment would break with even the slightest hum.

I felt my heartbeat mixed with hers. I lifted my arms slowly and wrapped them around her, holding her tight to my chest. I lowered my head near the crook of her neck and nuzzled her hair. She smelled like earth smells after the rain. So natural and so pacifying. She slowly released her grip, and I knew it was time to let her go. Her hands traveled from back to my chest as she distanced herself slightly. I felt the warmth of her hand on my beating heart. Few of her tendrils were still clinging on my t-shirt. She looked up at me, and I saw adoration for me in those easy-to-read eyes.

"This is your birthday gift. I can't give you anything more than this," she whispered. I lifted my hand and covered her hand that was rested on my heart.

"This means the world to me," I said. We looked at each other as the silence hummed with the desire. Before I did something I regretted, I removed my hand and took a step back.

"Goodnight, Riya," I said before I left her room.

CHAPTER 17

Down The Memory Lane

"Why do we need to shop? Don't they have shops in Moori?" Nitya asked me as I tied the laces of her shoes.

"They do have, Princess. But we won't get time as we have to make the biggest snowman there," I said, and she seemed somewhat satisfied with my answer. She was insisting on going to the temple with my mother because she wanted to tell her friends about the trip to Mussoorie the next day, but instead, she had to accompany us to the shopping. Riya didn't argue when Nitya and I made a plan to Mussoorie in front of her the previous day, and we took it as a positive sign. Perhaps the child inside her was excited to experience the mountains, but her grown-up exterior was too adamant about showing any kind of excitement.

Riya wanted to buy some more clothes and snow gloves for Nitya. That was why we decided to go shopping. Nitya jumped off the chair as she saw Riya coming out of the room.

"Maa, we are leaving. Shall I drop you to the temple?" I said loudly to my mother.

"No. I have canceled my plans," she answered from her room, and it had me worried. She never canceled her trip to temple, no matter what. I strolled towards her room and found her sitting on the edge of the bed, staring at my father's picture—her usual place whenever she was in tension.

"What happened, Maa?" I asked.

"Nothing. Just not feeling well," she said, and I reflexively touched her forehead. It was cold with slight perspiration.

"Let me check your blood pressure," I asked and was about to get up when she held my hand.

"I have a bad feeling; As if something ominous is about to happen," she said.

"Oh! Maa, stop worrying too much! Nothing is going to happen! Come with us. I will drop you to the temple. Once there, you will feel better," I said, and she caressed my head.

"Just be careful," she said, and I smiled at her.

After dropping my mother to the temple, we headed to the Shopping Mall. This time Riya strictly warned Nitya that if she got down the carriage, she wouldn't take her to Mussoorie, and surprisingly Nitya complied. Half an hour later, Riya appeared and tossed a Green sweater in my direction.

"Here, try this one," she said.

"Are you buying me this?" I teased her.

"Yes, I am! Consider it a gift as I am going to join my new job from coming Monday," she smiled with her chin up. Laughing, I strolled towards changing room and tried the sweater.

"Hey, It's a perfect fit. How do you know my size?" I asked, coming out of the trial room.

"The credit goes to the great shopping connoisseur," she replied tugging on her jacket collar in self-appreciation, making me laugh. After the shopping Nitya wanted to have Pizza, so we went to the food court. Riya offered to buy the Pizza, and I didn't stop her. She loved paying the bills, and I let her. I made Nitya sit on a high chair while I sat on the stool chair. Hugging her chair, I rested my head on her lap.

Heaven.

That's how it felt when those little hands caressed my head. I closed my eyes and reveled in the feel of a motherly touch from a four-year-old. I smiled, realizing how beautiful it is to have a daughter. She kissed the top of my head and rested her head on mine. Her kind and innocent gesture had my heart melted. *I am never going to let them go away from me, no matter what.* I promised myself silently.

"Hey, sleepy heads, get up. Pizza is here," Riya's voice rang in my ears. I lifted my head laughing as Nitya shrieked looking at Big Pizza box. We exited the shopping mall after feasting on Pizza. Riya held all the shopping bags, while I picked Nitya, as she was tired and sleepy. I smiled at Riya as I saw her rounding the car to sit on the passenger seat. I opened the back door and made Nitya sit on the back seat. Kissing her cheek, I closed the door. I had just turned when I heard the earsplitting shot. I was instantly jerked back to my car. I widened my eyes as everything started looking hazy. I listened to the rustling as people around me began to run. A sudden surge of panic I felt in my gut, something was wrong.

Riya.

I turned my head to look at her and found her beautiful face stricken with horror. I wanted to ask what was wrong, but before I could, she threw the bags in her hands on the road and rushed to me crying. I noticed other hazy figures running towards me. Why did my shoulder felt like as if someone had stabbed me there?

Nitya.

Her thought made me turn my head to look inside the car. I felt my body too heavy to move, but somehow, I tried to peep inside the car. All I could see on the window was blood! A lot of blood! My heart started pounding erratically as I pushed back the panic and wiped the window with my hand to make sure Nitya was all right. Her eyes filled with the terror stared back at me. I tried to smile to reassure her, as she started pounding the door.

I couldn't.

I felt my skin too tight to move any muscle. Something was terribly wrong, but before I could conjecture what it was, everything turned black as I hit the road.

Down The Memory Lane

I opened my eyes, my eyelids felt heavy and swollen. I tried to move but couldn't. It felt like my whole body was made of stone. The white and blank ceiling glared at me as I looked up—this wasn't my home. I tried to examine my surroundings and found so many tubes coming out and in my body—I was in the ICU. What happened to me? Why couldn't I see anyone around?

Maa, Riya, Nitya.

Shit!

I couldn't just lie there when the women in my life might be in danger. I needed to get up, and I needed to see them. But despite all my effort, I couldn't move an inch. My chest blazed with helplessness. I tried to calm down, yet the desperation clung to my heart. What if something happened to them? *Riya. Nitya.* They were with me. I was supposed to protect them, but I couldn't. I had seen Riya running towards me, but she never reached. The stricken face of Nitya flashed in front of my eyes, and I lost all the semblance of composure. What if someone had taken them away from me? I couldn't bear the thought. I couldn't lose them. I tried to shout, but no voice came out of my mouth. Sharp pain in my shoulder took over me, and I again saw the haze that took me to the darkness slowly........Again.

Present Day

September 2019

Grand Finale, *The Singing Star*

Mumbai

My hand reflexively moves to my shoulder where a bullet had hit me years ago, as my mind plays that dreadful incident. Some pains always linger to your body no matter how much time had passed. It's just that with the time you learn to mask them well. The only relief was Nitya and Riya weren't harmed in that incident. But I knew this incident would be etched forever in our minds and would haunt us for life. I feel her hand above my hand on my shoulder; I look at her and know that she knows what all is going in my mind. She gives me a reassuring smile despite the pain she had endured herself. Her pain is much more than mine, yet she never fails to comfort me. She entwines her fingers with mine and rests it over my lap. Leaning towards me, she kisses on the scar on my shoulder over my suit jacket, making my heart melt. How does she always know when and what I am thinking? How does she understand me so well? Tightening my grip on her hand, I bring it to my mouth and gently kiss on the back of her hand.

CHAPTER 19

Down The Memory Lane

My eyelids fluttered open to the barren ceiling of the room. It wasn't my room. My room had elaborated plaster ceiling. As I observed my obscure surroundings, panic crept over me. Where the hell was I? Gazing around the room, I tried getting my bearings, but the anxiety kept rising. I remembered what happened to me last, and again, the petrified faces of Riya and Nitya flashed in front of me. Where were they? I tried to get up but felt my body paralyzed. Unable to handle the apprehension, I started calling out incoherently. I heard the clatter at the door and turned my gaze and found Riya standing there. Relief cascaded down my body at her sight, even though she looked crestfallen. I looked down and found that she had dropped something she had brought with her. I saw her slowly falling to the floor on her knees. Her hands rested on her thighs as she tried to breathe and then I heard her sobbing. She quickly recovered and then picked up the bag off the floor and started gathering the things that had fallen out of it.

"Hey," I said, trying to smile but felt my skin stretchy, as if I had a certain swelling over my face. She came near me and sat on the stool beside my bed. Holding my hand in hers, she rested her head over it as she cried her heart out.

"Talk to me, Riya," I said, but she didn't respond. I sighed. I could understand her state, so I let her take her time. I tried to lift my left hand but couldn't. I needed to know what had exactly happened. It seemed like a whirlwind—One moment we all were smiling, and next moment we all were terrified. A bustle at the door made me turn my head there, but Riya didn't budge. A nurse entered and greeted me with a smile. She quickly came to my side and checked the parameter in the monitors installed at my side. I closed my eyes, suddenly feeling exhausted.

"I almost lost you," Riya whispered, and I looked at her. I couldn't see her face as she had turned it opposite to my direction. I looked around and found that the nurse had already left.

"You have got me, dear. Tell me, what happened?" I said and heard her sobbing again.

"Welcome back, my son. You scared us all," I looked at the door to see Chauhan uncle entering the room. Riya quickly bolted up and wiped her face with the back of her hand as she heard his voice. He strolled to stand beside my bed. Riya promptly got up and offered him the seat. Sitting there, he looked at me.

"How are you doing now?" he asked. He was my father's best friend. We used to meet frequently, but now it had been almost a year I had seen him.

"I am good, Uncle. How are you?" I asked, and his eyes crinkled as he smiled in response. His greying hair and brown complexion accentuated his puritanical outlook.

"Now tell me what happened?" he asked, and I snickered.

"That's what I am dying to know what happened? We were coming back to our car. Then I heard a shot. All I remember next is panicked faces and lot of blood," I said, reliving that dreadful incident again in my head. My body shuddered as Nitya's face flashed in front of me. I instantly looked at Riya.

"Where is Nitya? How is she?" I couldn't help asking.

"She is good. A little shaken but recovering," Riya said, and I saw her eyes welling up again.

"Where is she?" I asked again. I needed to know if she was safe.

"At home. With Aunty," she replied, but her answer couldn't bait my anxiety.

"Alone?" I asked, but before she could answer, Chauhan uncle chimed in.

"Don't worry, son. We have organized a special security team there, they are safe," he said, and I felt my body relaxing a bit, but I still needed to see them with my eyes.

"You were shot in the car parking—The bullet had hit your left shoulder. You were lucky that it didn't do any damage to your heart," he said. That's what I had assumed, but who could do that. Was it the people who were after Riya? But they couldn't reach us this early. No one knew that Riya left with me that day… except for that receptionist. But if it were they, why they didn't take Riya and Nitya with them? I tried to contemplate the situation. My eyes darted at Riya, and I found her hands trembling as she looked down discomfited. Shit! She was blaming herself for this. I needed to soothe her and tell her that it had nothing to do with her.

"Did you have any idea, who could do that? They could have done more damage, but seeing people running towards you made them flee." Chauhan uncle asked, and I knew he was watching my every reaction warily. He was no longer a sweet, loving uncle at the moment, but an austere Police officer on duty. I needed to mask whatever was going in my head.

"I have no idea," I said, and he gauged my response looking at me. He then averted his eyes at Riya.

"Can I talk to him in private?" he asked Riya in a clipped voice. Nodding once, she left the room.

"Who is this girl?" he asked me once Riya was out.

"She is family," my answer was curt.

"Really? I needed to know everything about her, Ady. The attackers weren't local. And I strongly suspect it had something to do with her. Don't hide anything, Son," He said. He looked stern and puritanical.

"Stop doubting her Uncle. It had nothing to do with her," I tried to hide everything; though a part of me wanted to tell him. I knew it was the right way to go about it. But I needed to have Riya's consent before I said anything. I doubted that Uncle hadn't questioned her before, and if she didn't tell him anything, that means she wouldn't want me to spill.

"Can we talk later? I am tired," I said, and Uncle nodded. He left the room after some more small talk. Once he was gone, Riya entered again. She sat beside me with her head down. Why wasn't she talking to me?

"What's wrong, Riya? Talk to me," I said, unable to keep my concern.

"It's all because of me," she said, and a lone tear rolled down her cheek.

"It's not you, Riya! Don't blame yourself. Being in a business, we have our share of nemesis," I lied. The nemesis were the last thing we had earned. My father had always been polite and helpful and had gained a reputation here. I knew well, people who knew us would never think to hurt us. But I couldn't say this to her. She was already distressed, and I didn't want her to blame herself. But I needed to talk to her.

"Chauhan Uncle asked about you, but I didn't say anything," I said and looked at her to gauge her reaction. She looked down at her clasped hands.

"I know," she mumbled. "They have already interrogated us several times. He is suspicious," she whispered, ashamed.

And I wanted her to draw in my arms and tell her none of this was her mistake.

"I think we should tell him about our situation. He isn't the one to run to them with this information. I have known him since I was born. He will be at our side no matter what," I tried to elucidate.

"I know! He was quite distraught when he came here, but I need some time. They are dangerous people, Adyant. They have their ways to play with the law and system. Telling more people will be like putting their lives in danger. Can you give me some time to think?" she said, and I nodded. She held my hand in hers. Looking down at our connection, she whispered, "I was so scared. I thought I had lost you,"

"I was scared too. I did think that I lost you two," I shuddered even thinking about that situation. I looked at her and felt relieved. She was there in front of me, sound and safe, and that's what mattered. Now I just had to make sure they were protected. She had warned me before, too, but I didn't assume it to be this worse. But now I was prepared, and I wouldn't hesitate involving police also if she agreed. Her consent was important. She had trusted police once, and instead of protecting her and her child, they betrayed her. It was hard for her to trust them again, and I understood that. But we weren't equipped to fight with them without involving the police. We were raised with high morals while they were inhuman and unethical. They could go to any extent for what they wanted. I looked at Riya and found her lost in her thoughts. I studied her profile. She looked tired and dejected, I had never seen her like that before.

"Hey, I am ok. Stop worrying," I said to appease her. She smiled in response, but it didn't reach her eyes. Neither it curved her lips in a way that made it enthralling.

"Any idea when they are going to discharge me?" I asked, and she straightened her back.

"The Doctor said once you are conscious, he will observe for another twenty-four hours then you may go home," she said and looked down. I closed my eyes, suddenly feeling exhausted and dizzy.

"For how much time I had been unconscious?" I asked with my eyes closed.

"Around twenty hours," she answered.

"And again I feel like sleeping," I said, and my eyelids felt so heavy to open.

"It's perfectly fine. The nurse just injected the dose of painkiller, and the doctor said it's normal for you to feel sleepy after the dose," I vaguely registered what she all said, but I did feel the caress of her hand over my forehead. With a grin on my face, I fell into a deep slumber. With her presence around me, life felt like heaven even when the circumstances screamed hell.

CHAPTER 20

Down The Memory Lane

"Your discharge slip is ready. I have explained the medicines and the precautions to Riya and your mother. Take good care of yourself and do visit if you have any problem. Having slight fever and drowsiness is normal," the doctor said as I got up to sit on the wheelchair. I could walk because it was my shoulder that was injured, not the legs, but no one listened to me, so I had to capitulate. Everyone had come to the hospital to take me home. My mother didn't say much except caressing my head and kissing my forehead. She wiped her eyes occasionally, that told me she was crying. *I have a bad feeling*. Her words reverberated in my head. Are mothers blessed with an extraordinary sense to foresee the danger to their children? I smiled at her, and she smiled back with her pursed lips as more tears fell. I blinked to ensure her I was perfectly fine. Nitya was there too, but she didn't talk to me. In fact, she didn't speak to anyone at all. I didn't hear her chirpy voice, and that killed me. It was sad that a little child had to go through all this. I smiled at her, but all she did was hiding behind my mother. Perhaps she was handling the trauma in her own way.

Soon we were at home, and I was lying on my own bed. After lunch, I dozed off for some time. When I opened my eyes next, I saw Nitya playing on the carpet beneath.

"Hey, Princess, what are you doing here?" I asked, and she instantly stood up. I didn't mean to scare her, but she looked stricken all of a sudden. When she didn't say anything, I added, "What's wrong, Princess? Why don't you talk to me?" She strolled to stand at the side of my bed. "I am no more a Princess," she said with the big tears in her eyes.

"Why do you say that?" I asked, suddenly fighting the urge to take her in my arms, but I felt pain when I tried to move it.

"I don't want to play that game. I don't want to get you hurt," she said as she sobbed silently. My heart crumbled at the thought of how badly this incident had impacted her. Trust me, its heart wrenching seeing a child crying without the sound. I wished it was in our hands to stop the game anytime, but life has its own rules. The game life plays ends only after death. Once we cross a level, life waits to throw another curve at the next level.

"Oh! Dear, it doesn't matter if we are playing that game or not, you will always be my Princess," I said and tapped my right hand on the bed. "Come sit here with me," I said, and she shook her head. "Mumma says I can't sit there. I may hurt you," she said.

"You can never hurt me, Princess. Come here," I compelled, and she obeyed. I talked to her and played games with her, and soon she was her usual self.

I saw my mother entering the room when Nitya was giggling at my stupid joke. She smiled at Nitya and told her to go and play outside. I instantly knew she wanted to talk about something that she couldn't speak in front of Nitya. I prepared myself for the explanation. My instincts told it had something to do with Riya. I had noticed in the hospital too. My mother wasn't as cordial with Riya as before. Once Nitya was out, she dragged the chair from the corner and sat beside me.

"How are you feeling now?" she asked.

"Much better," I replied, propping my weight on right hand in an attempt to sit. She quickly came to my side and helped me to get up. Once she was satisfied with my new position, she took her seat.

"It's all my fault," she said as her eyes started brimming again. "I shouldn't have let her stay," she added and inhaled sharply.

"What are you talking about?" I said, scowling.

"See, Ady, I don't want to be rude, but she has to go. Your life is too precious, and I can't take the risk," she continued. Her voice wavered, and eyes welled up again that she hastily wiped with her fingers.

"It has nothing to do with Riya, Maa," I said. I didn't know it was true or not, but until proved it was wrong to blame her for this. And even if it was because of her situation, then also it didn't mean she was the culprit.

"It has. An enemy is the last thing we have ever earned, and you know that. See, Ady, I am not telling you to abandon her and let her fight it on her own. But at least send her away from here. We will bear all of her responsibilities. We will hire top-class security for her. And if you still aren't satisfied, we may arrange to get her settled in some other country, far away from any danger. But she can't stay here. We make toys; we are the people who think twice before killing even an ant. You think we are equipped to fight those cold-blooded people?" she talked without pausing for a breath, and I knew she was determined. I tried to speak something, but she held up her hand.

"Only thing I know is your life is too precious, and she is not worth it," she said with the finality. Without listening to anything from me, she scampered out of my room. Exasperated, I closed my eyes. I knew it was dangerous not only for me but for Riya also. After all, those people were after her and not me. How could I let her go in this kind of situation? Moreover, I couldn't imagine my life without both of them.

I picked up my phone and switched it on. There could be some warning or threat that I might have missed before. That could give me an idea about who could do that to me. Numerous notifications flashed on my screen as it woke up. I huffed realizing that now I would have to explain each and everything to everyone. I typed a small message and sent it to everyone who had called or messaged me. I made a call to Shaun, Nik, Mani and also to my *Riyaz* manager, Yash, to let them know I was okay. Next, I called Mrs Singh, my manager of Delhi *TingTong* branch. After making another few calls to friends and relatives, I stared at my next contact in a quandary. I didn't want to talk to her, but she was a friend and had called several times, so I decided to call Ekta. Her phone kept ringing, but no one picked. I sighed in relief as the operator informed in a mechanical voice about her unavailability. I was so overwhelmed to talk to her right now, and my missed call would ensure that I called her back. But I wasn't that lucky because my phone vibrated just a minute after.

"Hey, Ekta, before you start, let me tell you that. I am perfectly fine, and there's nothing to worry," I said and heard her sobbing. I felt instantly bad for being rude to her, even though it was just in my head when she had only been concerned about my well-being.

"Hey, stop crying! I am perfectly fine. Save them for later when I actually die," I said to make her smile, but it did the opposite. "Never say that," she replied and sobbed harder.

"Please stop crying, Ekta! I am tired of seeing women crying around me," I jibed.

"It's all my mistake," she said, and I shook my head. Why were all the women around me taking all this on themselves?

"It has nothing to do with you," I said and realized she wasn't listening.

"All I wanted was her to be out of your life," she blubbered, and I felt tongue-tied. What did she mean by that?

"What did you do Ekta?" I asked, holding my breath.

"I anonymously informed her husband about her whereabouts?" she sniveled, and it became impossible for me to contain my anger.

"Do you have any idea what you have done? How the hell did you know about her husband?" I barked through my gritted teeth. I couldn't know anything about him until Riya told me herself. How could Ekta have known about Riya's husband?

"She wasn't Esha's direct friend, but she was a friend of a friend. It wasn't that difficult," she said, and I clenched my teeth in an attempt to stop myself saying anything that I would regret later.

"I am sorry, Ady. I didn't know those people were dangerous. I thought they would come and take her away from you. I am telling you all this so that you know who attacked you and be careful in the future. Stay away from her, Ady. If possible, send her as far as you can," she said, and I instantly knew who crammed this thought in my mother's head.

"Thanks for your fake concern, Ekta. But I can take care of her and myself too. I love her! Did you hear that? I love her! And she is my responsibility now," I deliberately said that to hurt her.

"And one more thing, this is the last time we are talking. Have a great life ahead," I said and disconnected the line. I felt like screaming, but instead, I closed my eyes and tried to calm my nerves because I had a lot of thinking to do. Leaving this matter to resolve by its own would be nonsense. Not after knowing that Yogit could reach to Riya anytime. I felt a slight relief that there was security outside my house. I had to inform this to Riya so that she could be more careful. I winced realizing that this would confirm her that everything that happened to me was because of her. I was still engrossed in my thinking when I heard the screech of the chair.

"Is it hurting?" I opened my eyes to see Riya sitting on the same chair my mother had been sitting a few moments ago. She mistook my pained expression for my injury. She picked the medicine box from the side table and took out a few medicines for me.

"Medicine time," she said, smiling at me. I could see the red rims of her eyes that told me she had been crying. Her hair was a complete mess, and she hadn't changed her dress since yesterday. I also noticed the darkness around her eyes. Her hands trembled when she took out the tablets from the leaf. I decided not to scare her by telling her about Yogit. She was safe for tonight and tomorrow I was going to take this case to the police. He had tried to kill me, and that would be enough reason to file a complaint against him. Then maybe we could talk and resolve the matter because at this moment he would do anything to save his public image, and with my huge fan following, I could surely damage it beyond repair.

"I am okay, Riya, and it wasn't because of you," I tried to appease her, even though my heart was pacing because of my own trepidation. Somewhere I knew that the next few days were going to be an ordeal. She smiled and bobbled her head, saying, "I know." A clear indication she didn't want to discuss anything about it. And I too decided to dodge the topic. It was better to talk about something else that could lighten her mood. At least for tonight, because the next few days promised the choppy waters ahead.

"I couldn't take Nitya to see snow," I said grimacing, to divert her mind.

"It's ok, you will have plenty of time later," she said, and hope started building inside me. We would have plenty of time later. Smiling at the thought, I asked her, "Was Nitya complaining about this?"

"No. She was quite shaken. She couldn't sleep that whole night, and still shudders and cries in her sleep remembering that dreadful incident," she said, looking at the wall blankly.

Her face was devoid of any emotion. "I am so sorry. She had to go through all this," I said feeling sorry for that effervescent little girl.

"She is not even four, yet she had already seen a lot. Her own people had betrayed her. Is it all because she is my daughter? Remember? Once you asked me how I feel about my birth parents? I hate them. I hate them from all my heart. Not because of what they did to me, but what my daughter will have to go through because of their deeds. She deserves a better life. She should be going to some play school like any other normal child, but all she is doing is running to save her life," she said, and tears appeared in her eyes.

"She loves you, Adyant! Perhaps more than she loves me. You can't imagine what she went through seeing you lying lifeless there with blood scattered everywhere," she said as she rubbed her tear-streaked face.

"All I wanted was Nitya to have a normal life, normal expectations from life and real dreams. Do you know why I ran from Yogit? Not because I was scared for my life, but the thought that she would end up alone in the world if they didn't kill her. I don't want her to have my fate," she snivelled, and I instantly felt her pain. "I never tell her anything against her father, because I want her to trust people, like any other child of her age does. I want her to have faith in love so that she doesn't freak out when true love enters her life, and she pushes it away just because she thinks she is not good enough. She is not worthy of someone too good. I don't want her to repeat my mistakes," she said lost in her own thought as tears kept rolling down her cheeks. Did she realize what had she just said? Was it about Nitya? Or was it about her… and me? Did she freak out that day and pushed me away? Unable to hold my racing heart with every beat, I cupped her face with my uninjured hand and forced her to look at me. My shoulder started hurting instantly because of the strain, but I didn't care.

"What did you say? You freaked out?" I said, and her eyes widened in realization.

"You freaked out? And I spent all these years thinking that you didn't like me. That you didn't love me. You freaked out? Do you realize how much time we have lost just because of your stupid thought that you weren't worthy?" I grimaced thinking we wouldn't have been in this situation if she had given me the slightest semblance of her thoughts that day. She acted as if she was making excuses to push me away because I wasn't her type.

"You freaked out?" I laughed mirthlessly shaking my head. "There were so many things I wanted to do with you. I wanted you by my side on all the gigs. I wanted you to clap and cheer for me on all the award ceremonies. I wanted to explore the world with you, and not just the oceans, deserts and mountains. And now you are telling me you freaked out? Oh, Riya! There wasn't a single day when I didn't think about you; when I didn't look for you in the crowd. I didn't change my number thinking just in case you felt like calling me. Even though you were never there, I always felt you around. And you freaked out?" I said as an exasperated tear escaped my eye. My voice was laced with anger. Anger that I didn't fight enough for her. Anger that she pushed me away and I left her without a second glance. Life would have been so different if I had tried a little more. I walked away from her without realizing that she was expecting me to fight for her a little harder.

"I was scared, Adyant. I was too young and too stupid and had sworn not to trust anyone then. I freaked out because no one had ever done anything to make me feel that special. You know, the moment you sang that song I felt like you were talking to me. As if you were grateful having found me," she said, and I whispered bobbling my head, "I was! I really was."

"And then it hit me that I must stay away from you. You seemed like dangerous territory," she laughed through her tears, and I rubbed my thumb over her cheek, smiling at her gloomily.

"Because the first time in life, I felt like I could love you without any expectation, without any purpose. I could love you even if I had to burn myself to make it happen. And I wasn't used to that kind of feeling. It freaked me out. I haven't loved anyone in my life more than myself. And I couldn't bear the thought of you hurting me at some point of life. I was just saving myself. I wasn't that girl someone would love to introduce to their family, and you too had realized that," she paused as I shook my head in disapproval.

"What made you think so?" I asked. I was never ashamed of her. I loved her the way she was. How could she even think that I would not introduce her to my family?

"You didn't try after I said *no* and you left without glancing back," she said, and I couldn't hold my incredulity, Yes! I left without trying that day because I didn't want to foist myself on her. And moreover, how could she think that way when she clearly said she didn't want me?

Perhaps, she was testing me, and I failed her. The realization hit me like a punch in the gut. Considering she got ditched by almost everyone whom she deemed her own, it was quite possible.

"There are two kinds of love, Adyant. First one keeps you entertained, and another one feeds your soul. You may survive the loss of the first one, but the loss of the latter makes you dead from inside. I saw the second one in your eyes that day, and I wasn't ready for it and freaked out. I wanted to run away from you, and I did. But then I realized I had to meet you for the last time. So that I could etch your picture in my mind. But now I have realized how wrong I was—you would have fought for me. You would have done anything to make sure that our love kept feeding our souls," she said, and I nodded.

"We can still start afresh, Riya. It's not too late. I will fight to my death if you are by my side," I said, and she nodded.

"Now no more these hiding games. We are going to fight head-on. I am going to involve the police," I said determined, and she smiled in agreement. I didn't know how I was going to fight with him, but one thing I had learned was—If you are determined, impossible is just a dictionary word.

"Whatever you feel is appropriate. Now take these medicines. These will calm you to have a good sleep," she said, handing me the tablets. I didn't want to have them. I knew it was going to make me sleep. After Ekta's confession, how could I have taken them, knowing fully well that my whole family was in danger? But Riya was adamant, and despite my refusal, I had to take them. She helped me to recline on the bed again and pulled the quilt to cover me. She cupped the side of my face. Leaning to me, she kissed my forehead and then my cheek.

"Good Night," she said, and then left the room without glancing back. The medicines started working as I felt the weight on my eyelids, but before it could dope me to sleep, I called Chauhan Uncle to ensure the security was tight.

Present Day

September 2019

Grand Finale, *The Singing Star*

Mumbai

"Hold your heart guys, we are going to announce the result now," Host announces. Parth, one of the three finalists, is already eliminated, and now there are just the two, Nitya and Samarth. "Let's welcome our judges again on the stage," the hostess says, and the whole arena thunders with the loud applause. I see the judges walking on the stage. I hear the thumping of my heart loud and clear. Once the judges are on stage, they invite the guest of the evening, which is the famous film star. Judges hand over him a card in which the winner's name is written. He opens the card, and everything starts to happen in slow motion, and I curse him in my head for taking so much time to open a damn card. He reads the result and smiles. He comes forward and stands between Nitya and Samarth.

"Are you ready to know the winner of *The Singing Star*," he shouts, and the audience replies boisterously. He takes Nitya hands in his left and Samarth's in his right and starts waving them up and down. The audience becomes silent, and the auditorium reverberates with the sound of a thumping heartbeat.

Dhak-Dhak...

Dhak-Dhak...

Dhak-Dhak...

I glance at my wife sitting beside me and find her as anxious as I am. She takes my hand in hers and leans in my direction to say something in my ear.

"This is the moment, Ady. Look, her dream is about to come true, which is your dream too. Now you have someone to take your place in your band. And soon we will have someone to look after *TingTong* too" she says, resting her another hand on the small bulge of her stomach, she is five months pregnant. I lean to her and kiss her temple.

"What about the Just-In-Case one?" I tease her to get some respite from the tension.

"Don't worry Mr Adyant Lohani. I will make sure he or she likes being a businessman. You won't need the spare one," she says with a sly smile on her face.

CHAPTER 21

Down The Memory Lane

A loud husky laugh woke me up, I smiled with my eyes still closed. It was the same laugh that had enticed me six years ago. I opened my eyes and squinted because of the light in the room. Riya had left the tubelight on in case I needed something. Through my squinted eyes, I saw Riya laughing, throwing her head back. My smile widened as I dragged my self with my right hand up to sit.

"What?" I asked, taking her in. I felt the instant nostalgia as I saw her dressed in the saree we had purchased together six years ago. She was looking younger and precisely the same as she looked that day. Her hair were open in loose curls. And she radiated the same glow she had on her six years back.

"You snore while you sleep," she said and laughed again.

"Do I?" I said in amusement. "By the way, why are you dressed?" I asked, narrowing my eyes at her.

"Because I wanted to make this moment special," she said, tucking her hair behind her ears. I noticed the way her cheeks reddened.

"Come here," I said, folding my legs and tapping the space my legs had vacated gesturing her to sit. She complied.

"What is so special about this moment?" I asked. She sat in front of me, and with her eyes frozen on the bed, she whispered, "I couldn't say you then, but I want you to know that I loved you." I swallowed the lump of bulging emotions in my throat. It seemed like it had been forever since I waited for this moment. Closing my eyes, I inhaled sharply. I knew she was waiting for my response, but I didn't say anything. She made me wait for years; I could make her wait for a few seconds. See, I had learned the retaliation from her. I smiled at the thought. Opening my eyes, I placed my finger under her chin and made her look at me.

"Marry me," I said and saw her eyes widening in response, and then she laughed.

"Aren't we already married in a way?" she said, and I looked at her, confused.

"Marriage is not just about tying a knot; rather, it is about having a real connection. Marriage is not about living together in one home; rather it is about living in each other's heart, no matter how far the physical distance is. And I am damn sure, we are going to stay forever in each other's heart, even if it is the last time we see each other," she said, and I looked back and forth in her eyes. She didn't seem worried about our situation. All the signs of distress I had noticed sometime before were gone. She had a glint in her eyes that said she was happy and at peace. I opened my mouth to say something, but she hushed me by placing her index finger on my lips.

"It's enough now. You need to sleep," she said as she helped me lie on the bed again. My eyes did feel heavy as I closed them and then she kissed my forehead and started to leave.

"Where are you going?" I asked, forcing myself to keep my eyes open.

"To God. I want to thank him for letting me live this moment," she smiled.

"What time it is?" I asked.

"Five in the morning," she said glancing at the wall clock. I followed her gaze and found it was exactly five in the morning. She might be referring to worshipping with my mother.

"Come soon," I said and closed my eyes again. She again came near me and kissed my forehead. My mind vaguely registered something she said afterward as I slowly drifted to sleep.

Present Day

September 2019

Grand Finale, *The Singing Star*

Mumbai

"And the Little star of *The Singing Star* is—" the guest of the evening waves his hands holding the hands of the finalist, and then he lifts Nitya's hand and exclaims, "Nitya Lohani!"

And I can't hear anything as the whole auditorium starts whooping and cheering with the claps and hoots. Everyone stands on their seats to see the final moments on the stage. I purse my lips in an attempt to keep my emotions in check while my eyes well with the tears. I clap my hands as hard as it is possible.

"Come, they are inviting us on the stage," my wife says, and I shook my head. Too overwhelmed to spur any word out of my mouth.

"You go. She needs you," I say.

"She needs you more," she replies, turning towards me and clutching my shoulder.

"Nitya told me not to show my face until she invites me on the stage," I say trying hard not to let my tears fall in front of her.

"Okay," she says and strolls towards the stage holding border of her saree gracefully. I see her disappearing in the crowd as she walks away from me, and a familiar feeling claw my heart, taking me back to that fateful day.

CHAPTER 22

Down The Memory Lane

White.

It's white all around, and the only thing I am hearing is giggles. Riya's giggles. Nitya's giggles. The sky is extraordinarily blue as if God has painted it with his own divine hands. I see the snow sprinkled all over the trees, making a layer of a cozy blanket around them.

Mountains.

That's where we are! I smile as I see Riya helping Nitya to make the biggest snowman ever. Nitya is jumping because she wants to touch the snowman's nose. I want to go there and help her, but I can't move. I don't know what is holding me back. So I watch them from afar.

My angels.

Dressed in all white, they both are looking celestial. I keep looking at them as they finish the snowman. Nitya starts running, and Riya follows her, giggling. I love this sound, and it's better than any music I have created till date. I need to run because I can't bear not to have them in front of my eyes. And suddenly I am free. I run after them. And all of a sudden, my surroundings are gradually changing. The snow that has covered the land a moment ago turns into the sand. The mountains covered with snow slowly transforms into the dunes.

Desert.

We are in a Desert now. Riya lifts Nitya in her arms and twirls her. Nitya is giggling. Riya is giggling. I take a step to move towards them, and I am stuck again. I can't go near them. I am unable to play with them. I call them, but they both are so engrossed, they aren't listening to my plea. But I am happy because they are happy. Even though it's torture not be able to touch them. Riya makes Nitya stand on her feet, and she giggles as she falls because of giddiness. She stands and runs again. I look up at the sky and see that it's the same blue from the mountains. I look down as a wave makes my feet sink and squish into the wet sand, and I realize that it's no longer a desert. I smile and stare as I see Riya and Nitya giggling and throwing seawater on each other.

Ocean.

We are on a beach. The sun is descending slowly into the sea. Riya and Nitya both are drenched yet they can't stop playing. Riya looks at me this time and gestures me to come join them. I try to move my feet, and this time, I succeed. I run towards them. Riya takes Nitya in her lap, and after kissing her cheeks and forehead, she gives her to me. I happily spread my arms for my princess. I kiss her and nuzzle her stomach the way she loves, and she giggles again. I look at Riya and see her walking away with her front towards me. The warm and salty waft blows her hair as she locks her eyes with mine and waves her hand at Nitya and me. Then she slowly turns and keeps walking away. I behold her as she gradually disappears with the fading sun. Where is she going? I ask myself, but I don't care. I have Nitya, and as long as I have her, Riya will come back to me. No matter how far she goes. I kiss Nitya's forehead closing my eyes, and when I open them, I am in my own room — lying on my own bed.

I winced, as I felt the pain in my shoulder. I heard my phone buzzing on the side table. Picking it up, I saw Chauhan uncle's number on it. Why was he calling me this early in the morning? I glanced at the watch and saw it was quarter past six in the morning. Supporting myself on my uninjured arm, I sat on my bed. I took his call.

"Good morning, Uncle," I said.

"How are you now?"

"I am good,"

"Do you have any link with Yogit Pradhan?" he asked, coming straight to the point, and I instantly broke out in cold sweat. How did he know?

"Umm...what happened?" I asked, holding my breath. I had a sudden urge to run and see if Riya and Nitya were fine, but I had met her just an hour before. The thought made me relax.

"He was assassinated yesterday," he said, and I couldn't believe my ears. I sat abruptly on the bed without caring for the excruciating pain in my shoulder.

"What?" I asked, shocked. But an instant relief cascaded my body when I gave it a second thought.

"Yes, he is dead,"

"Wow... I mean that's sad," I said. How would Riya react to this? A thought crossed my mind. Even though that man was nothing but a fiend in her life, she loved him.

"Hmm... Don't you want to know who killed him?" he hauled me out of my reverie.

"Who?"

"The girl at your home, what was her name?" he said, and I laughed.

"Riya. You aren't going to spare her, are you? Well! It can't be her. Because she is here with me,"

"Right now?" he asked, and a chill ran down my spine.

"No. But a few moments ago, she was here," I said, and my voice wavered showing my uncertainty, anxiety started gnawing my chest.

"It's not possible, Ady. Because she too died this morning," he said, and I could breathe no longer. I felt like someone sucked all the oxygen from my room. I started to feel sick.

"Are you insane? What are you talking about?" I raised my voice an octave.

"I don't know if you are aware or not, but she was armed. Yesterday night, around eleven, she shot him right in the chest and he died instantly. In return, she was shot by his bodyguards. She was alive when the ambulance brought her to the hospital, but couldn't survive as her lungs were damaged. Do you have any idea what connection she had with him?" he asked, and I was no longer listening to him.

"That can't be true," I clicked the call off and held my head.

She was here with me yesterday night when we confessed our feelings. Then she was here again early this morning when I asked her to marry me. Then again we were on vacation. Mountains. Deserts. And Oceans. I hard-pressed my ears as it started buzzing, muting all other sounds around me. I was too disoriented to realize what was a dream and what was a reality. The sedatives I had taken seemed to have messed up my brain. I bolted up from my bed and ran to Riya's room. My shoulder screamed with the pain, but I had no time to tend it. I yanked the door open and found Nitya curled up on one side of the bed in a deep sleep. There was no sign of Riya. I ran to check the washroom, and again, she wasn't there. Panic started clawing its fingers around my throat and stifled me. I rushed out calling her name. My mother came out of her room.

"What's wrong?" she asked.

"Where is Riya?"

"I don't know. Isn't she in her room? I haven't seen her since yesterday."

"Didn't she come to you this morning for Puja?"

"No. She didn't," she said, and I saw my worry reflecting on her face too.

"What happened, Ady?" she asked with fear etched all over her face. I kept looking at her. How could I have answered when I had no idea what had happened last night? My throat constricted in pain as I tried to spurt words out of my mouth. I felt like I had lost my ability to speak. I swallowed in an attempt to hold my emotions. I tried hard to keep sanity in check, but it was far out of my hand. I fell on my knees as my legs gave up. My mother rushed to me and started consoling me incessantly. I looked at my phone that I had tightly clenched in my hand as if it was the only source to reach her. I redialed Chauhan uncle's number.

"Which hospital?" I asked as he picked up the phone. A tormented sob choked off in my throat. I gripped the phone tightly against my ear as I heard him answer. I was unable to comprehend how it was even possible. Did I miss something when I was talking to her yesterday? Was she confessing her feelings or just bidding good-bye? I gathered myself before grief started to engulf my sanity. I needed to reach her as soon as possible.

I didn't know what all happened next few minutes. How I reached the hospital. I was too numb to feel anything happening around me. Chauhan Uncle was already there when I entered the hospital—The same hospital where she had walked beside me a day before when I got discharged.

"Do you want to identify the body?" he asked me, and a big ball of anxiety had my stomach roiled, and I felt queasy. I glared at him for being so insensitive. How could he call her a *body* when he knew her name well? My eyes were burning, but not a single tear escaped.

"You said there was tight security outside, then how did they take her?" I asked, looking blankly at the board above the reception area.

"She willingly went out of the house. There was no pressure on her, and moreover, the security was for your protection, not for her. You never mentioned she had any kind of threat," I closed my eyes, wishing I had told him everything a day before.

"Now will you tell what all this is about?" he asked, offering me to sit on the benches near the waiting area. I told him everything I knew. Her facial expressions played in my mind like a movie when she had told me all this.

I will never hear her voice again, the thought made my body tremble. Was it really happening? Or was I still in a dream?

Dream! Yes, it could be a dream.

Hope started building in my chest. Closing my eyes, I said a little prayer. All I wanted it to be a nightmare I would soon wake up from.

"I see, now I understand everything," he said, contemplating. I looked in his direction as I voiced my thought, "What do you mean?"

"We have strict orders not to let any word out or issue any statement regarding this incident, and also they are stalling the investigation. I think they are worried about the proofs that Riya had. An investigation may unveil the things that can put an end to their political career, as they have no idea to what extent the proofs can damage their reputation. Perhaps they are more worried to save their prestige than mourning over their dead son," he said, shaking his head.

"Do you want to see the body?" he asked again. Did I want? Or rather I would picture her happy and content as I had seen her in the morning. Was it just my dream? Why did it feel so real? Her reply reverberated in my head when I had asked her where was she going. *To God. To thank him for letting me live this moment.* My body shook from the realness of the reverie.

"When can I take her with me?" I asked, unable to call her a *body*.

"I can't tell you that we will have to wait till the next orders," he said huffing. "I will make sure, that your name doesn't get involved in all this," he said. Did he know my life was involved in it? And now with her, a part of me had also died. I closed my eyes and first tear of grief cascaded down my cheek. Once the first tear made its way, I was no longer in a state to control the unbroken stream that followed.

Riya was gone!

Hiding my face in my hands, I let myself break. I couldn't gather the courage to see her. Perhaps not seeing her would keep her alive in my memories. At least for some time, because sooner or later, I would have to face the reality. My phone buzzed in my hand, and I glanced at it to find the call from my mother. How was I going to explain all this to her? My body shuddered as I thought about Nitya. How would I tell her? She wasn't able to handle what happened to me. How would she take her mother's death? Tears welled in my eyes again thinking about that little girl. I had to get to her as soon as possible. I bolted up and came out of the stifling hospital environment, while a part of me wanted to stay there. Riya was alone, but the little girl at home needed me more.

"Please, God! Stop doing this to her and have a little mercy on that little soul." I mumbled a prayer, looking up at the sky. As I slid inside the car, a surge of rage gushed in my body. How could she do this to me? Why didn't she tell me anything? Or was I mistaken? Did he threaten her to come out? What else could make her go out of the home at that hour? There were so many questions that would never be answered. The only person who could answer was gone. With heaviness in my chest, I entered my home. My mother was already crying. Perhaps she had gotten the news from Chauhan uncle.

"Nitya?" I asked my mother.

"Still sleeping. I didn't know how to break the news to her, so I let her sleep," she said as the tears flooded her eyes. I sat on the sofa, resting my hands over my knees. Everything seemed hollow around as if Riya had taken away the soul of this house along with her. I glanced up and saw Nitya standing near the door of her room. I spread my arms and gestured her to come to me. My eyes welled with the tears again as I tried to smile. I wished I could fast forward the next few hours… or better rewind a few hours of my life.

She sauntered towards me and stood in between my legs. Wiping my tears with her little hands, she said, "I know you miss Mumma, but don't cry. That's a rule of the game,"

I looked at her, dumbfounded. "Mumma told me this. Not to cry ever, she told me that now it's her time to hide, and we are not supposed to cry over her. She has to do it so that the bad people don't hurt you again," she said as if she wasn't affected by the absence of her mother.

"Won't you miss her?" I asked as my eyes glossed again.

"I will! But we both want to protect you. She also told me to take care of you," she said.

"When did she tell you all this?" I asked feeling cheated that she prepared Nitya for the departure but didn't utter a word to me.

"Yesterday, at storytime," she said, and then her expression changed to a shock as if she suddenly remembered something.

"I forgot. Mumma left you a letter," she said and rushed inside her room, and was back in a jiffy holding a folded white paper.

"This," she extended the letter towards me. "She told me to give this to you in the morning. She has written all the rules for you," she elucidated and turned to my mother. "I am hungry," she said, and my mother gathered Nitya in her arms.

I unfolded the letter and started reading it.

Dear Adyant,

I know you must be quite angry with me right now, but that's what I always do. I do stupid things, and that's why I was never apt for you. There will be thousands of questions running in your mind right now, and I couldn't leave without answering all of them. I know how it feels to live with so many unanswered questions.

After you were admitted to the hospital, Yogit approached me. Not directly but through a phone call. He was so wary about his reputation that he dreaded getting seeing with me. He has threatened me with your life, and this time, I can't take any risk. Your mother is right, your life is too precious, and I am not worth it.

I closed my eyes, realizing that she had heard the conversation with my mother the previous day. I grimaced thinking that her last thought was she wasn't worthy, and I did nothing to expunge it, rather my conversation with my mother confirmed this because I didn't correct my mother when she had said that. I clapped my eyes again to the letter to read it further.

I have two options now, either lay down arms or take up arms. I have decided to go for the latter, while, to him, I am pretending the former. If he thinks I will capitulate without fighting back, he certainly doesn't know me well. I had bargained the time I spent with you after the discharge, and now it's over. I need to go to him. I need to end all this. I won't lie that I am not scared, but I have no regrets. It's best for everyone.

Reading this, now I realized. There were so many signs. How could I be so ignorant not to see them? She was scared. It was evident on her face. When was the last time I had seen her so crestfallen? Never. Even in the worst of the worst situation, she was always positive and smiling. How could I miss it in her gestures? She was being threatened and went through it all alone. Why couldn't she trust me? Did she think that I wouldn't be able to fight him? That I wouldn't be able to protect her? I closed my eyes momentarily to absorb this thought. I held up the letter in front of my eyes and started reading it further.

Please don't hate me, and don't you dare to take it upon you. I know you would have done anything to keep us safe. For Nitya and me you are the knight in the shining armor, it's just, I am not that princess who is going to hide behind you and see your armor getting dented silently. I would rather stand in front of you and fight to keep the shine of your armor. And don't blame God either for all this. Just like before, he has again given a pen in my hand. It's just me who is too tired to write the next chapter. It's my mess, Adyant, and I have to clean it. I trust you. That's why I am leaving Nitya with you. Take care of her, and don't spoil her too much.

I smiled through my tears, realizing how well she knew me. She answered everything as if she could read my mind. She was gone. How am I supposed to live now? Did she realize she ended me the moment she decided to end her?

I know it's going to hurt you for a while, but trust me, everything will be fine. Don't dishearten yourself by seeking a happy ending in our relationship, because it's always the story that ends not the relationship.

My eyes widened in the realization that these were the words she had whispered in my ear before I dozed off in the morning. Did she actually come to meet me before she left the world? Did she request God to let her live that moment? Keeping the havoc in my mind aside, I concentrated on her letter.

Moreover, our story was never the one. We both had different stories. It's just our paths crossed when one of us was going through the rough patch, and instead of ignoring, as most of the people do, we helped each other. It doesn't mean we have to have a happy ending. Moreover, it's wrong to call an end happy or sad. An end has no emotions, but life has, and it must go on. It's the end of my story, not yours.

You have a heart of pure gold and some lucky girl who is as pure as you deserve to own that. Not someone like me with so much selfishness and baggage.

Wistfully, I rub the spot on the paper where the ink was spread with my thumb. Perhaps, it was her teardrop that had cockled that area. I brought it to my mouth and kissed it as my own tears fell on it. She wasn't selfish at all; she was just trying to make her place in this selfish world. I wished I could make her understand that, but now it was too late. I would never see her again. The thought cocooned my heart in the darkness of grief once again.

I was never the one for you. You are yet to find the girl born for you. Do find her and fall in love with her. Don't keep her deprived of love God has written in her destiny. I was just a character in your story to propel you towards the goal, while she is the protagonist—the one to give your story the happy ending. And trust me, if everything goes as planned, it will be a happy ending for me as well. I will be leaving the world with a man I loved—the one who promised me forever. We are going to sort out all our differences in another world, far from this materialistic world, that keep us luring with the dreams so much that we forget there are things beyond the money, power, and fame. My daughter is in the hands of one who loves her more than her own parents. The one who is going to give her a normal life and real dreams. The onc who would go to any extent to protect her, and won't hesitate to hire goons if need be. What else can I ask for?

Always remember, Adyant. Never take your life for granted. Neither the loved ones you are blessed with. Don't poison your life mourning over the loss of someone who wasn't meant to stay forever. Rather cherish the moments you got to spend with them during their stay. I don't know what rambling mess I have jotted on paper. All I want is you to live your life merrily, and I will be merrier in another world. I am going to end this journey here. I hope you will forgive me.

Take care of yourself.

Love,

Riya

Present Day

September 2019

Grand Finale, *The Singing Star*

Mumbai

I feel a warm tear rolling down my cheek. I am so overwhelmed right now that I have no idea if it was the tear of glee or the nostalgia I have just relived in my head. I wiped it hastily. I keep clapping my hands pouring out all my jumbled emotions—happiness, proud, anger, and grief.

Riya.

No matter where I am or what I do, she is always present in my thoughts. She appeared in my life like a fallen angel from the sky, and just like that one day, she was gone. I can count the days I had spent with her on my fingers, yet it felt like she was born for me. After her death, the case was dismissed immediately portraying Yogit as a martyr that he died saving a woman's life from goons. It did bring their party a lot of sympathies, and they won the elections. I wanted to fight against their claim, but that would have tarnished Riya's image only because it was Riya who had attacked Yogit first. There was no way I could prove that Riya was Yogit's wife without involving Nitya, which I didn't want. That little girl had already gone through enough, I didn't want to suffer her anymore.

I was ready to fight for Nitya in case someone came claiming for her custody, but no one cared to look for that poor soul. It still scares me thinking that what would have happened had Nitya wasn't with me. I legally adopted Nitya after all the formalities, and now she is my rightful daughter.

I try to focus on the moment. I see Nitya holding a big dummy Cheque of rupees ten lakhs. I see my wife smiling and wiping her tears occasionally.

After Riya left me all shattered, I engrossed myself in looking after Nitya so much that how days got blurred I had no idea. She was my only connection to Riya. I released my pent-up emotions in the lyrics of my songs. It was my way to heal myself from the loss of love that was never mine to begin with.

I kept jotting my fear, my loneliness, and my frustrations in my songs without realizing that somewhere far away, they were healing a heart that was way more broken than mine. Naina, she had lost her fiancé just a day before her wedding. My songs gave her the comfort that she was seeking desperately. How funny is that we find comfort in someone else's words and think that they would know all the answers to the turmoil we are going through, but the reality is far away! She emailed me and wrote everything that had bugged her mind. She emptied her self in that email. She poured out everything— Her love for her fiancé, her regret for forcing him to meet her the day he died in the accident on the way, her guilt that she was the reason he was no more, and also how my songs made her feel alive momentarily. Getting these kinds of emails from fans were the usual thing for me. And truth be told, I never cared to read them. But it was the subject line that made me click on that email.

All these oceans, deserts and mountains, don't make me endure the pain. What am I supposed to do?

It was in reference to an inconsequential line in my song that held lots of emotions for me. After reading her email, something clicked inside me. She had asked all those questions that I was finding the answers for myself. I responded to that mail, and slowly, we started exchanging the emails regularly. After being in touch with each other through the mails for three years, we finally met when we performed in a concert in her city. I smile reminiscing that day. Riya was right. Not every person we meet is meant to stay in our life forever. Some are just to leave their mark and propel us further towards the goal. But life goes on, with or without them. We continue meeting new people and explore new relations. It's wrong to keep yourself clung to one loss when life has so much to offer on every step. I read somewhere that if you keep your eyes on one closed door for too long, you will certainly miss the next door that God has opened for you. No one can indeed fill the void Riya left in my heart, but Naina taught me how to live again with that emptiness. We found solace in each other's grief, having found someone who could understand the feelings. Let's say as time passed we fell in love with the understanding we had for each other's first love. We got married because we felt safe with each other. None of us tried to drag out each other from the past, because we knew well that we valued our past as much as we regarded present. We both moved on together, being each other's strength when one of us felt weak.

I clear my vision and focus on the stage as now Nitya is holding the mike in her hand. The host asks her to share her feelings, and she is so wheezy that all we hear on the mike is her heavy breathing.

"Thank you all. I am feeling so happy. It's like a dream come true. I have no words..." she rambles. Keeping her hand on her heart, she takes deep breaths, while Naina holds her shoulders and supports her.

"I want to dedicate this—" she lifts the trophy in her hand "—to my Papa. He is not just my father but also my mentor, my best friend, my guide, my everything. You must be wondering why he wasn't present in any of the previous shows. The reason was I had asked him to stay away because I wanted to do it myself. I didn't want to influence the public voting by revealing his name. And it has nothing to do with my ego or self-respect. He has always been my backbone. My biggest strength. But whenever I look into his eyes, I always see myself as his weakness. Can you imagine he still ties my shoelace because he thinks I will fall? And I am thirteen now," she laughs, and the audience also laughs with her.

"I just wanted to prove to him that I can be his strength too. I am capable of fighting not only my battles, but I can support him too. I love you, Papa," she said and turned her face to wipe her tears.

Papa

I still get the goosebumps when she calls me that. I still remember the first day to her playschool, where for the first time she had introduced me as *Papa* to her friends and teachers. It was an innocent gesture as every other child was introducing the same way, but for me, that day had been a joy to behold. I had felt so glorious, so honored that moment as if I was sitting on the top of the world. I smile, realizing that my little girl is no longer little now. Look at her, how she is talking all grown up! And how could she say that? Doesn't she know she still can't tie her laces properly? She turned to face the audience again.

"Today, I want to introduce—" she shook her head "—No. He doesn't need any introduction," she smiles and after a hiatus adds, "Put your hands together to welcome Adyant Lohani, my father, on the stage," she says, and the auditorium fills with the hushed whispers and few claps.

"I guess you haven't recognized him. Let me call him by the name you know him better, Ady from *Riyaz*," she repeats, and this time the whole auditorium roars with the loud applause. People call my name as I walk through the aisle. Some even come forward for a selfie. Waving at them, I jog to the stage. Nitya meets me halfway and hugs me.

Lifting her in my arms, I twirl her as she giggles. *See, she has a real dream, and she has already started the journey.* I say in my heart looking up, wishing that Riya must be watching this moment somewhere from another world. They say an average human spends roughly 692, 040 hours on this earth, yet there are only a few life-changing moments that remain etched in our heart forever. I will forever be grateful to the universe for blessing me with those eight hours with her. Otherwise, I would have never known what a beautiful soul Riya was!

"I am so proud of you," I mouth to Nitya before kissing her forehead. I look at Naina standing beside us, all in tears. I extend my one arm to invite her to the family hug. She rushes to us, and we all bind ourselves in a tight embrace.

Epilogue

Somewhere In Future

I pace apprehensively in the drawing-room looking at the text Nitya has sent me. Naina's neck move side to side as her eyes follow my movement. I can't believe Nitya could do this to me. She knows well I hated that boy. I again stare at her message that says: *I am sorry, Papa. I lied to you about my trip to Goa with friends. I am here to marry Samarth. Don't try to pull any stunt, because in the next five minutes we will be married legally.*

"Stop Ady, you running here, and there isn't going to stop her marrying that boy," Naina says, and I stand resting my hands on my hips. I exhale loudly, exasperated.

"She can't do this to me, I know that boy is making her do all this," I say.

"No. They are in love, and she would have invited you to the wedding had you not smothered her," Naina says.

"What did you say? I had smothered her? Me? He is not good for Nitya. Remember? She lied to me because of him," I counter.

"Not because of him, Ady. It was because of you, she would have told you about her date had you not been so uptight about Samarth," Naina rises from her seat and stands in front of me.

"She doesn't know what's right and wrong," I say.

"She is no longer a child; she is twenty-four now, and she knows Samarth since she participated in that reality show," she retorts, and I reminisce them hugging each other after Nitya won the title and he didn't. I should have stopped them right then.

"But I can't accept that boy. She used to love me, and because of him, she started hiding things from me," How can I forget that she signed a music album with that boy without my knowledge!

"I know what you are referring to. But for once be honest Adyant, would you have allowed her to sign that album? And to top that you started spying on her. What was she supposed to do?" she comes closer to me and holds my hand, "Trust me, she still loves you. It's not easy for her either, but you left her with no option." I cringe at her words. There must be a way I could stop them. I think about informing the police, but they are consenting adults. My phone buzzes in my hand, and I see Nitya's face on it. I smile even though I am angry. She looks exactly like Riya except Nitya has straightened her hair permanently. I quickly pick up the phone. Naina gestures me to keep it on speaker, and I comply. My heart sinks when I hear Nitya sobbing.

Shit! I knew he wasn't a good boy. I give Naina knowing look, and she rolls her eyes.

"Did he hurt you? I am going to kill him with my bare hands," I say and hear Nitya groaning.

"Stop it, Papa! He never makes me cry, on the other hand, he always offers me a shoulder when you make me cry," she didn't just say that!

"I make you cry?" I ask, shocked.

"Yes! You do, why do I love you so much?" she sobs again, thawing my heart.

"I couldn't do it, Papa, I can't do it without you, because I want you in my wedding happy and excited," she says.

"Come home, and we will talk about it,"

"No! we will be doing it! I am coming back home. And no more drama and manipulations, Papa. Samarth loves you too, you are his idol so stop behaving like a child" she chastises.

"Okay," I say. Will I ever get used to being reprimanded by the women in my life? I huff.

Acknowledgement

My first thanks to my grandparents for their forever blessings, my Father-in-Law, my parents and my Naniji for their endless love and support. Anita Vatsal for always encouraging me. Ritu di, Richa, Nitasha for providing valuable suggestions, thank you from the bottom of my heart. You know how much your opinion matters. Anita, Pragati and Priti for always being there.

My sincere thanks to team invincible for making this happen, especially Mr Ajay Setia, and my editor Pooja Mishra for being so supportive.

My gratitude to all my relatives and friends for teaching me the invaluable lessons of life, which helped me in portraying the characters the way I did. I can't mention all the names here, but you all know how blessed I feel to have you in my life.

People always ask me how could I manage to write with two kids around, and the reason is that I am blessed with the sweetest and most supportive kids in the world, Agastya and Advitya.

And lastly, Amol Malik—nothing would have been possible without you. I really can't thank you enough for letting me spread my wings and follow my dreams.

Author's note

Never take anything for granted. Your reality might be someone's unfulfilled dream.

A special thanks to you for reading this story and I would really feel happy to reccive your review. Short or long doesn't matter, but do post them. You may connect with me through my social media handles:

Facebook: www.facebook.com/anjum.a.malik

Instagram: @anjumawasthi

Twitter: @anjum_awasthi

Email: anjumawasthi@gmail.com

Also By the Author

1. ***The Twist of Fate***

A young and vivacious girl, Raahi is all set to live her dream in a big city. A crucl twist of fate and her world starts collapsing around her. Aadit, a business analyst in New York, is effervescent and full of life. Or at least that's what he shows to the world, but deep down he is still struggling with his own demons. The fate interweaves their lives together and just when a bond is about to bloom, life throws another curve at them. They start drifting apart completely oblivious to what fate has in store for them. The Twist of Fate is a heartfelt and enamored tale of the entangled emotions of love that promises to keep your eyes glued to its pages.

2. ***The Day He Was Gone***

Reeva Panchal has had a traumatizing past, but she is trying to build up her life again from scratch with her skill in the art. When she receives a surprise marriage proposal from the wealthy hotelier Agnivesh Solanki, she can't help but feel odd about it even though her parents are insistent that she agrees to it. With Agnivesh's entry into her life, all her problems seem to alleviate at an unrealistic pace, even though Agnivesh continues to exude a dark aura for her. What unfolds is a series of unprecedented events where relations are broken, mistakes are made and the past is dug up to destroy as well as heal.